HEALED SOULS SERIES

BOOK ONE

Because Of Yesterday

Grecia Chasteen

My memories are like scars that never fade. But even scars become stories.

And these stories, when held with love, become a source of healing: Light!

Who Am I?

I am the silence that swallowed screams.

I am the question no one asked,

I am a female who has experienced many lives in one lifetime,

The twists and turns, the ups and downs.

I am a female with many identities... spiritual bi-racial lesbian.

I am a mother who is still learning to be a parent.

I am a sister and a daughter.

I am someone's ex-wife and ex-lover, but I am hoping to be someone's

Dream come true.

I may even be someone's enemy, the shadow to their awakening.

My love flows like oceans within me, but I often drown in fear.

I am always dreaming big and questioning every step...unsure if it's right.

I am running from failure and slipping on mistakes. I am a female who has found comfort in solitude,

But aches for connection.

I cry in silence,

While speaking in song,

I have so many things to say, yet nothing comes out.

I believe God has a purpose for me, unsure what it is, but I continue to patiently wait.

I am a female, better yet… I am a

woman becoming.

A soul who's searching.

A heart that's healing.

A lover ready to love fully.

I am me!

A Word Before We Begin

This book is not just a reflection of what I survived. It's a soul journey.

I return to these words now, years later, with clearer eyes and a softer heart.

Not to rewrite the past… But to

release it.

For her. For me. For you.

I hope my story helps with your journey.

Pain came early. Healing would have to wait.

SESSION ONE

Part One: Opening the Door

I sit in my car, staring at the white building like it's a mirror ready to show me parts of myself I've been avoiding. My stomach twists. When I made this appointment, I had a thousand things to say, but now that I'm here, my mind feels blank. What if I open my mouth and everything I've been holding in spills out? What if I finally tell the truth and it changes how I see my whole life? How can a stranger help me with my problems?

Why am I paying someone to listen to me talk?

Do I not have any support?

Am I that alone?

Maybe I'll just do this one session, check the box that says I tried, and move on. At least then I can tell my family I gave it a shot. Maybe I won't have to admit that I'm scared to be seen. Scared that if I start talking... I won't stop. Or worse, that I'll talk and still feel empty. I grab my purse and step out of the car. "Geez, it feels like I'm carrying around luggage instead of a purse," I mutter. "Great, now I'm talking out loud to myself before seeing a therapist, how ironic." I shake my head as I shut the door and walk toward the building.

I glanced at the sky. "God… if you're listening, don't let me fall apart in there."

I turn around to the parking lot, debating just leaving again, and see a bird landing on the hood of my car. I pause to watch it. For a second, I wonder if it's a sign, or maybe just a bird, and I'm digging too deep. Either way, I open the door to the building and take a deep breath.

Inside, I fill out the paperwork the receptionist gives me, then follow her to the corner office down the hall. The small office is organized, with college degrees in brown frames hanging on the wall. The scent of vanilla oil drifts from a small warmer. I sit on the couch and glance out the window at another bird perched in a nearby tree. If I were a bird, I think, life might be easier, or at least I'd feel free. I thought to myself.

"Hello, my name is Ms. Jones. How are you today?" she asks with a warm smile as she shuts the door and takes a seat across from me. She smiles gently. "What brings you in for therapy?"

"I guess I came because… I'm going through something with my partner right now," I begin, shifting in my seat. "And… I don't really know what to do. I just feel stuck."

I pause, before adding softly, "And honestly, my family keeps hinting that maybe I've got some things from my past I haven't dealt with."

I shrug. "So, I figured... maybe it's time to talk to someone. Even if I don't know where to start."

Ms. Jones nods. "That's a big thing to admit, especially when you're feeling stuck. Can I ask, have you ever been to therapy before?"

"No." I shake my head. "This is my first experience or my first time," I respond, not sure of the correct way to answer without sounding silly.

"That's perfectly okay," she says gently. "I do want to let you know that everything we talk about here is confidential, unless you say something that makes me believe you might hurt yourself or someone else. In that case, I'd need to reach out for help, just to make sure you're safe, but I want you to feel comfortable and know this is a safe space. With that said, let's revisit your comment regarding your family... do you feel like your past might be affecting what you're going through right now?" She opens her notepad and looks at me with kind eyes.

I pause, eyes fixed on a spot on the floor, then glance up. "I don't believe so," I say slowly. "I don't really think about my past. And honestly, my past shouldn't affect my present... right?"

I force a laugh, but it feels thin. "This is about a relationship, not some deep mommy and daddy issues or childhood trauma." I shrug like I'm brushing it off, but my voice goes softer. "At least... I don't think it is."

"I want to know as much as you want to share," she replies with another warm smile.

"Umm... well, I'm not used to talking about myself. Where should I start?"

"Start from the beginning."

"My life hasn't been perfect, but I guess it's been okay. I try to stay positive, you know? I always remember that someone is going through something worse than me, so I shouldn't complain too much, you know?"

She nods.

"I guess I'll start with a story my mother told me. I was four months old. She said I was a happy baby until one day I seemed different. I just stopped laughing and smiling. My mom rushed me to the children's hospital, explaining that something wasn't right. The

3

doctors ran tests and sent us home. The next day, she returned, still convinced something was wrong. They did additional bloodwork and sent us home again. Then they called urgently: 'Bring her back immediately.'

It turns out that I was losing my white blood cells. They wanted me to be admitted. But my mom didn't trust them; she demanded they give her the medicine, and she took me home. She gave me the medicine herself and took me back and forth until I was cleared."

"How did hearing that story make you feel?" Ms. Jones asks.

"I guess... I feel like my mom saved my life because she trusted her gut."

"Would you say she was protective of you?"

"I guess so. Never thought of it that way."

"How about we revisit your first memory? Something that you remember experiencing."

"It's not a great one."

"Often, our first memory is impactful, whether joyful or traumatic. It's something our mind decides to keep and store for later. Tell me what you stored as your first memory."

"Okay. I was four years old. I was watching TV with some family friends, my sister, and I. I can remember someone pulling a blanket over us, meaning them and me, and then they climbed on top of me. I can remember the pressure of them against my body, and the floor hurting my back. I remember turning my head and looking toward the small kitchen where my mom and her friend sat, laughing. I watched her laughing and smiling with them as I silently begged her to look at me. She never did. My tears fell quietly as I lay there, waiting for it to stop."

"Nadia, I am sorry you had to experience that at such a young age. That moment must've been difficult to feel like she wasn't there to protect you that time."

"Yeah... I guess if you look at it that way. Almost like she protected me during a time I can't remember, and the time I do, she wasn't there."

"That's an interesting way of looking at those moments. I want to revisit those emotions, but I would like to ask, do you remember who this person was that did this to you as a child?"

"I don't remember the face. I think I blocked it out. But I assumed it was Frank. He was about seven years older than me."

"Was Frank the son of your mom's friend that she was laughing with in the kitchen? You assumed it was him, so was this something that happened more than once?"

"Yes, he was. And yes... that wasn't the only time, just the first that I remember."

"Did he come over often, or did you go to his house a lot?" Ms. Jones asked.

"Yes. We were like family. I can also clearly remember one time we were building tents using blankets and sheets. Linda, my younger sister, and I started filling the tents with our dolls and stuffed animals. Frank said that we were married, and the babies that I had were our children. I told him I was a single mommy, like my mom. He got upset with me for saying that. He crawled into my tent and said we were married."

Ms. Jones listens intently, nodding as I continue.

"He said we needed to make more babies, and he lay on top of me, attempting to have sex. I was about six years old. When he finished, he said he was done playing, and he left the tent. I pulled my pants up and just lay there silently."

"Did you tell anyone?"

"No. I didn't want to upset my mom. I learned at a very young age that she was sensitive. I felt like I had to protect her, but there was one time I tried to tell her."

"What happened when you tried?"

"I was crying on the top bunk after another incident that had taken place with Frank. My mom heard, came in, and asked what was wrong. I almost said it... But I realized I was telling her everything in my head, even though no words came out. She had asked me again what was wrong after the long pause. I told her I missed my dad. She said, 'Everything will be okay.' And for that moment... I believed her, although I used her words for the situation with Frank, not missing my dad."

Part Two: When the Body Remembers

"Did the sexual abuse happen often?" Ms. Jones asks.

"I can't remember every incident, but there is another time that stands out more than the others. One night, Frank watched my sister and me while our mom was out. We played and laughed; Frank used to play some fun games when we were younger, when we were really playing. But one night, we spent a couple of hours playing and building forts out of the couch pillows in the living room. Afterward, we lay down, and I remember feeling relief because when he fell asleep, it meant I was safe."

"Were you safe?" Ms. Jones softly asks.

I shook my head slowly. "I wasn't. I was half asleep when I heard him whisper to me to wake up. I pretended not to hear him and kept my eyes closed. After a few minutes, he rolled me on my back and pulled down my pants and panties. The cold air hit my skin, making me open my eyes and see only the glow of the streetlights filtering through the curtains. He put his head between my thighs, and I tensed up. That was something he had never done before, so I tried to wiggle away, but he held me down, tight.

I turned to check that my sister was still asleep. I didn't want her to wake up, so I tried to be silent and wait till it was over. Then something shifted. I started feeling this... warm sensation. It scared me. I felt a rush of emotions, and I hated it because it was confusing.

I jumped up, breaking free from his grip, grabbed my pants, and ran to the bathroom. I locked the door and cleaned myself with toilet paper, then climbed into the cold bathtub, curled into a ball. I didn't leave the bathroom that night. I was too scared. I hated the feeling that a part of me had... liked it. Frank knocked a few times, telling me to come out of the bathroom, but I stayed in there till I fell asleep."

"Let's take a deep breath together. That was a lot to unpack," Ms. Jones says, guiding me with a slow inhale and exhale.

"That's a very honest thing to admit," she adds gently. "You were a child. Your body reacts the way bodies are naturally wired to respond to stimulation, but that doesn't make what happened right. It was not your fault."

"I've always felt ashamed of that," I whisper, not wanting to make direct eye contact with her. "It's hard to say it out loud. Like... what kind of person am I if a part of me liked it?"

"Nadia, let's first recognize that you were a child, but you also learned at a very young age to be a survivor," she says firmly. "What you described is more common than you know and takes courage to recognize your emotions. Feeling stimulation doesn't mean you consented. You didn't choose it. It was forced on you. But your body responded the way it was wired to feel automatically. It doesn't make you guilty. It makes you human."

I sat there, stunned. I never thought about it that way before, and I let my breath exhale.

Ms. Jones broke the silence. "I'd like to ask: did you spend a lot of time around Frank? Was he an only child?"

"Our families were close, so we were around each other often. He had a few siblings, an older sister, Crystal, whom I used to wish was my sister."

"How was your relationship with Crystal?"

"I felt like I looked up to her. I always tried to be around her, which sometimes annoyed her, I think, but at that time, I didn't care. Sometimes she'd let me listen to music with her. I enjoyed those moments when she did acknowledge me. She always seemed so angry or sad, but I never fully understood why. I mainly remember wishing she would call me her little sister, but she never did. But I still followed her around, though." I smile.

"That sounds like an older sibling in many ways," Ms. Jones says. "Was Crystal ever around while the sexual abuse was going on?"

"No. I don't remember her being around. Something in the back of my mind wondered if she knew what was going on, but was scared to say something, I don't know. But I think if she were, she would've protected me, I would assume."

"Do you recall wanting to tell her what was going on?" Ms. Jones asks.

"I don't think so. There was a time when I thought my mom actually found out, though. I was about seven years old, and she took me to the clinic. While we were waiting, I kept trying to figure out why she was making me see the doctor, because I didn't feel sick.

As we sat in the waiting room, I assumed she had taken me because Frank wanted to make babies. I was trying to figure out how Mom knew, since I never told her. I was worried I was pregnant.

The nurse came out and called my name. The walk from the waiting room to the back office felt so long, and my stomach was in knots. I sat on the examining table and remembered hearing the doctor ask my mom what was going on. She said she had spotted a bald patch in my hair.

So now I'm pregnant and bald, I remember thinking to myself as a child." I laugh softly.

"As the exam continued, the doctor asked me if anyone had ever touched my private area. I said no. I wanted so badly to say yes and explain how it hurt and that I wished it would stop, but once again, no words came out except, "No."

I went back and forth to the doctor for tests. They checked me for leukemia, but the only conclusion the doctors came to was that my mother was braiding my hair too tightly."

Part Three: Love, Safety, and Secrets

"I'd like to shift a little. Was your father around during your childhood?"

"He was around some. I used to consider myself a 'daddy's girl.'"

"Why is that?"

"I loved spending time with him when we did. We used to play games on his waterbed all the time. There was this game where you had to add legs and eyes to a plastic bug. We played that game a lot. We also used to toss cards into his hat. Those were moments I got to enjoy being a child. I liked to think I was a 'daddy's girl' because I hoped he would protect me. I hated feeling like I was alone."

"What kept him from spending more time with you?"

"I'm not sure exactly, but I do know he was into drugs during that time. I don't remember seeing it many times, but I do remember one day, I was at his house, jumping on the waterbed, which he always told me not to do. As I jumped, I waited for him to come and tell me to stop, but he never did.

I decided to get out of bed to see what he was doing. I peeked into the kitchen and saw him at the table with a few of his friends. They were laughing and talking. I stood there, trying to see what they were looking at because they were all focused on something on the table. Then I saw my dad sniffing what looked like lines of baby powder.

I stood there for a while, hoping he would check on me, but he didn't. So, I went back to the bedroom and kept jumping on the waterbed."

"Do you remember how you felt standing there?" Ms. Jones asks.

"I don't remember what I felt standing there, but I do remember thinking I was invisible because no one looked at me."

"You mentioned not remembering many times. Is there another time that stands out when you witnessed the drug use?"

"Not that I remember clearly. There was a time my mom and I were watching TV, and a commercial came on about saying no to drugs. After it ended, I said, 'My daddy does that stuff.' After that, she didn't let me see him as much.

Another time, he was dating a woman with two kids, an older son, and a daughter my age. I spent a lot of that summer with them, and I loved it. It felt like a real family. I felt safe, and that made me happy. We'd play board games, rollerblade, and race around outside. We just got to be kids.

But one night, while we were asleep, a loud banging at the door woke us up. It was the police who wanted to search the house. We stayed in bed, pretending to be asleep. I remember the mom at the door telling them, 'They're asleep.' The cops still came in and shone a flashlight into our room, so I shut my eyes tight.

After they left, I heard the mom yelling at my dad, saying she had kids in the house and didn't want this to happen again. She let us stay the night since I was there, but we had to leave the next morning. I didn't want to sleep that night. I knew once I did, I'd wake up, and the only place I'd ever felt safe would be gone.

The next day, we left. I said goodbye to the kids. The mom called a few times afterward to check on me. Then one day, the calls stopped, and I never heard from them again."

"That's a lot to carry at such a young age. Were there any outlets you remember having during that time to release all that you were experiencing?"

"Well, for my tenth birthday, I was given a journal with a small combination lock. It was the first time I started putting my thoughts on paper. I didn't write much at first, just enough to say I was writing in it. But over time, it became a space where I could scream, cry, and even laugh.

For the first time, I had a voice. I could express how I felt, even if I didn't fully understand it. Writing has stayed with me over the years. I still have a few journals, and I've written some poetry too. What's interesting is that when I look back through them… I never mentioned Frank."

"Why do you think you didn't write about Frank?"

I paused, the words feeling heavy. "It was a secret. Something I never wanted to say out loud to anyone. No one knew what happened for years. Maybe I even wanted to keep it a secret from myself."

Ms. Jones looked at me as I spoke, not with judgment, but with something deeper. Presence.

I paused, the memory of it coming back to me, but with a sense of peace.

"Another outlet I had was the drill team," I added, shifting slightly in my seat, trying to shift the conversation. "It made me feel like I belonged. Like I was part of something. I loved being in a space where we all moved as one.

I think it also taught me to express myself through movement… since expressing myself with words wasn't always easy for me. There was something about hearing the music and letting it move through me, like my body could say what my voice couldn't."

She nodded, jotting something down. "Having an outlet is important," she said softly. "Even if it's not talking, just something that gives your mind space to breathe."

"Yeah, I can see that. Another way I used my journal was to stay awake until my mom arrived home. It was a way to pass the time, which kind of sounds silly saying out loud now."

"Why was it that you wanted to stay up until she came home?"

"To be honest, I was scared she wouldn't come back," I say, my voice softening. "I was afraid she'd leave us, and we'd be alone. And I guess… I felt like I had to look out for her. Every time my mom went out at night, my mind would start racing with all the bad things that could happen. And with every thought, I'd plan. Just in case."

I glanced at the floor. "Like if someone broke in to rob us, how would I protect Linda? What would I do to keep us safe?" I shrug, embarrassed, saying it out loud. "I just wanted to be ready. I know… it probably sounds weird."

Ms. Jones gently interrupts, her voice steady. "Why would you call yourself weird?"

She jots something down and looks up again. "It sounds like you were thinking adult thoughts at a child's age. You took on a lot of responsibility."

I nod slowly. "Yeah. I did."

"I always made sure my little sister, Linda, was taken care of. That she was happy and safe. Before she started school, I used to teach her what I learned in my classes. She was two grades below me, but when I came home from first grade, I'd play teacher. I wanted her to be prepared. School was hard for me. I'd mix things up. My spelling was awful, and math was even worse. I'd make little cheat sheets for tests, not because I didn't try, but because I didn't want to be laughed at for struggling."

I pause. "But the things I did understand, I made sure to teach Linda. I just wanted her to be smart. Smarter than me."

"With the abuse you were going through, it would have been normal for you to struggle in school, but it also sounds like there were some deeper learning challenges you were struggling with. Were you ever tested for dyslexia?" Ms. Jones asked while writing on her pad.

"No, I was never tested, but I do recall someone else asking me about that later in life also."

"Maybe that is something we can discuss more about if you would like to."

"Umm, okay."

"Did you have other family around while growing up?"

"Not really, at least not in the early years. I only remember being around my dad's family a couple of times. My maternal grandmother lived nearby, but we weren't allowed at her house because her husband was racist.

She would visit on Christmas and bring us gifts, but we didn't see her much until he passed away a few years later. My mom was part of a club, though, and they kind of became our family."

"What kind of club?"

"A motorcycle club."

"What was it like, having your mother in a motorcycle club?"

"It was fine, I guess. It gave us kids things to do, like parties and cookouts. A lot of times, we'd spend the night at each other's houses while our parents were out. There was a woman with four boys. We'd visit sometimes, but my sister and I hated going. One time, we were at her house, and Linda and I tried to stay in the front room with my mom. But she kept telling us to go play with the boys.

The boys wanted to play '10 minutes in the closet' with us. They said one of us had to go in with one of them. We said no, but they insisted. I agreed to go first, so Linda didn't have to. They shut the door behind us. I just kept thinking, they better not be messing with my little sister. The boy in the closet started touching me. I just stood there, numb, staring at the light coming through under the door, trying not to feel anything.

When I thought time was up, I tried to leave, but the other boys were holding the door shut. I could hear them laughing. I started to get hot and panicked. The boy tried to kiss me, but I kept dodging him. I finally got out, and then they said it was the next boy's turn to go in with one of us."

"Were you able to discuss that situation with your mother?"

"No, I did not tell her, nor did my sister."

"Did your sister go in?"

"No, I didn't want her to, so I went again. The two younger boys didn't want to play. Thank goodness!"

Part Four: Almost Safe

"Did you have many friends as a child?"

"I had a few, but only one meant more to me than she'll ever know."

"What do you mean?"

"In grade school, I didn't care for her at first. But one day, as we walked to the library, she pointed out that her house was nearby. That's when I realized she lived right across the street from me. After that, I asked if she wanted to come over and play.

The day she came over, Frank was there too. I noticed that with her around, he couldn't be alone with me. After that, she and I became best friends. We spent so much time together. The good thing was that we had more in common than I expected. It worked out for the best." I smile.

"So did the abuse stop once he had less opportunity to get you alone?"

"Yes... Well, it slowed down a lot. It still happened, but not as much. He started saying things like, 'You're just for practice,' and told me his girlfriend was better than me. I remember having mixed feelings when he whispered that in my ear."

"What kind of feelings?"

"Like confusion mixed with shame. I wondered if he made her do it, too, as he made me, or if she wanted to. Then I started thinking something must be wrong with me... like maybe I wasn't doing it right.

17

I think that's why, as an adult, I ask people if I'm decent or not. Sounds silly saying out loud, but there is truth there."

"You mean with sexual partners you've had as an adult?"

"Yes. I sometimes ask them to rate me. I've had this need to be the best, not to be seen as a failure. I guess this is a breakthrough, huh? Connecting a past situation to something in my present?" I say, half-smiling, thinking maybe this therapy stuff is actually working, a little.

"It sounds like a connection was just made." Ms. Jones says with a friendly smile. "With Frank telling you that you weren't as good as his girlfriend, do you think that pushed you to want to be a good sexual partner later in life?"

"Yeah, I guess. I don't like being told I'm bad at anything. And even though I never wanted him touching me, it still hurt my young pride when he said stuff like that. I know it sounds silly," I say, shaking my head a little.

"It doesn't sound silly. What I'm hearing from you is that you wanted people to be proud of you. Correct me if I'm wrong, but it sounds like you've spent much of your life trying to prove that your worth is stronger than your wounds, that if someone could see past the flaws, the pain, the moments you couldn't control… they'd finally see the good in you. And maybe, they'd stay."

"That's deep, Ms. Jones. I'm not even sure how to respond, but… you might be right. I guess I've always felt like if people saw my flaws, they wouldn't stay."

"Everyone has flaws. It's okay not to be the best at everything." She pauses for a moment, then asks gently, "How long after your friend came into the picture did the sexual abuse continue?"

"It finally stopped during my fourth-grade year. Then, at the beginning of fifth grade, we moved, which put distance between us.

My mom wanted a better neighborhood and more opportunities for us."

"Did you move far, or were you still close to your old neighborhood?" Ms. Jones asks.

"We moved to the other side of town. I went from a school that was predominantly Black to one where I could count the Black kids on both hands."

"How did you feel about the move?"

"I think the move was needed, so I was happy at first, especially being away from Frank. But the change was a culture shock. At my old school, I struggled with being 'too white.' But then at the new school, I struggled with being 'too Black.'"

"Was race an issue for you growing up?"

"I wouldn't say it was an issue, more like a struggle with fitting in. The new school was in a wealthier part of the city. On my first day, a girl stopped me in the lunchroom and said, 'Good, another one of us,' and invited me to her table. I remember thinking, so now I'm considered Black here and white at my old school. Race wasn't an issue for me, but it seemed to be an issue for everyone else. Like they needed to label me one way or the other, and that made me struggle. Not just fitting in but also accepting who I was. I wasn't trying to be all white or all Black, considering I was both, I was just trying to belong or feel accepted somewhere." Ms. Jones nods thoughtfully, giving me space to sit with my words. There's a quiet moment between us, not heavy, but reflective; like something important has been spoken into the room. Then she gently leans forward, shifting the conversation just enough to explore another piece of my story.

"Were you able to find acceptance at this new school?"

"Nope! I ended up having a huge crush on this redheaded white boy," I say, giggling.

"Did he know?"

"Oh, no! We were friends and talked a lot, but he only dated white girls, so I figured I didn't stand a chance. It was kind of the same with another white boy I had a crush on; he was one of the popular ones. I thought he liked me too; we'd flirt, always talk in class... but then he started dating this blonde-haired, blue-eyed girl.

Even one of the Black guys I liked ended up with a white girlfriend."

"So, you never told any of them how you felt?"

"Nope. Not at all!"

"Sounds like you kept a lot of your feelings bottled up," Ms. Jones says gently.

"I did. I wrote some of it down in my journal, and my journal became my best friend, like a place to express what I was feeling."

"Journaling is a powerful way to express your thoughts," she nods.

Part Five: The Echo of No

"How was home life for you during this time of trying to find yourself at a new school?"

"It was okay. My mom hung out with some of the people from the club, but not as much, so she was home more. A few men would come over to visit and help her with car maintenance. I always tried to figure out who her boyfriend was, only to realize she didn't do relationships; she just had 'friends'. The men were nice to us and would bring things to the home, such as groceries or toys for my sister and me. I can remember my mother telling my sister and me never to allow a man into your house empty-handed."

"What did she mean by that?"

"My understanding was that if a man came to visit, he needed to bring something such as a gift."

"Did you build any kind of relationship with any of the men your mother called friends?"

"Yes, there was one man I looked up to. Honestly, most of my mom's guy friends were great and sweet, except for one. He just lived in the wrong era of life, I think," I say, giggling, at the memory.

"He was older but wore rapper T-shirts and big African chains. He'd bring stuff when he came over, like cheeseburgers, and a case of beer, which wasn't for us. That friend didn't last long. He bugged my mom too much. She didn't care for pushy men, especially the ones who tried to pursue a relationship with her.

But Mr. C… he was different. He was the one I used to pretend to be my father because when he visited, which wasn't a lot but enough for me to know him, he took time to talk and listen to me. He bought me my first CD player for my birthday. I had asked for it, and he got it for me. I was so shocked. It wasn't just the gift; it was that he listened. He cared enough to get me something I specifically wanted. That meant everything to me because I always felt like no one heard me."

"He took the time to hear you?" Ms. Jones asks gently.

"Yes," I nod. "He made me feel seen… like I mattered. And that was a feeling I didn't realize I was starving for at such a young age."

"Is he still in your life?"

"No," I say, shaking my head.

"Why not if you don't mind me asking?"

"I'm not sure. Sometimes I feel it had to do with one night when my mom had friends over to play cards. She would let me stay up late sometimes and play cards with her and her friends. It was music blasting, people laughing, smoking cigarettes, and drinking beer, but I enjoyed it. I remember sipping on my juice and feeling like I belonged, which I always enjoyed these nights. But that night, she had a lot to drink, more than usual. Mr. C was there too. And out of nowhere, my mom blurted out, 'You know she wishes you were her dad.'

I froze. My face turned hot, and I tried to slide down my chair. Mr. C responded, 'Well, she has a dad. I wouldn't want to take his place.'

My mom laughed. 'He ain't no good.'

Everyone stared. I was no longer part of the group and became the little girl with no daddy. Not one of the adults anymore, just the kid at the grown-up table. I wanted to disappear.

Mr. C repeated, 'She has a dad. I couldn't take his place.'

I felt the tears rising and ran up the stairs so I wouldn't cry in front of everyone. I locked myself in the bathroom in hopes of disappearing. People knocked on the door to check on me, but I said nothing. Then I heard Mr. C's voice.

He asked me to open the door. I slowly cracked it open, and he reached for me. I hugged him.

He told me, 'You're a great kid. Anyone would be lucky to have you as a daughter. I just can't take that from your dad.'

His words felt good... but they also hurt. Deeply. For years, I blamed myself for why he stopped coming around. But later, I found out there were other reasons he and my mom stopped speaking, but I do feel that had something to do with it."

"That sounds like a traumatic moment for you," Ms. Jones says gently. "You finally felt connected to an adult and then felt the rejection. How do you feel speaking about it now?"

"I guess... a part of me still feels abandoned in a way since I never saw him again. He was the closest thing I ever had to a father figure back then. And now, thinking about it makes me emotional. I have no idea why I still feel sad about it, and that makes me mad at myself."

"Why are you becoming mad at yourself?"

"I shouldn't still feel sad over something that happened so long ago."

Ms. Jones leans in. "You're feeling sad because once again, someone you trusted couldn't fully show up for you. And that old pain is resurfacing. You don't have to shame yourself for still hurting. What if, right now, you chose to comfort that little girl inside you?"

I take a breath, trying to blink away the sting rising in my eyes.

"I don't do the crying thing," I say quickly. "Tears are a waste of time. They don't fix anything. They just leave you with a headache."

I try to smile, but it feels forced, tight, like putting on a mask. "I always say crying is like a fucking hangover."

I pause. "Sorry for the language. Cussing is kind of my second language."

"It's okay," Ms. Jones replies, offering a soft smile. "However, you need to express yourself; that is perfectly fine with me."

Part Six: The Back Pew

"What about a higher power?" she asks next. "Were you raised with any spiritual beliefs or religious background?"

"I went to the youth group at our church. I actually enjoyed it. The youth pastor made me feel like I belonged to something. I also liked the idea that there was something bigger than me out there. It was the church that ended up triggering my childhood trauma."

I pause, the memory stirring up old emotions I hadn't felt in a long time. "There was one night… a church lock-in. We played games and sang songs. Later, we all went into the sanctuary to watch a video and pray. I sat in the back pew by myself, which wasn't out of the ordinary for me because I liked being on the outside and observing, if that makes sense.

The video we watched was about sexual assault and how you should tell someone if it ever happens. And suddenly, everything came rushing back.

Frank- The blanket- The tent- The bathtub-

Memories I thought I'd buried came flooding in all at once. I wanted to run to the bathroom and cry, but I told myself, if you get up now, everyone will know. So, I stayed. Frozen. Replaying the trauma I buried as a child, hoping no one would see my secrets. When the video ended, I pretended to be tired so I could lie down alone, trying to hold it together. That night, I whispered a prayer: God, please help me make it through the night without falling apart.

And somehow, I did. But I didn't sleep much. I remember also asking myself if this was even real."

"That happens to many people who've experienced trauma," Ms. Jones says gently. "It's common to block out what happened sometimes for years until something triggers the memory. Then the floodgates open, bringing a rush of mixed emotions. In a way, we give ourselves amnesia because we don't know how else to cope. That could also explain why you never wrote about Frank in your journal; you didn't want to connect to what was going on at the time."

"Wow… that actually makes sense." I nod slowly, feeling the weight of it.

"I remember sitting there in church, like I couldn't breathe. That might've been my first anxiety attack. The video felt so long, and it kept repeating the same phrase: 'Tell someone.' I didn't. Instead, I asked God to help me hold it together until I was alone. And God did help me make it through that night without anyone suspecting anything. I made it through the video… and even the group discussion after. I didn't fall apart. I didn't say a word. My secret stayed safe with me. But I didn't realize then that keeping it safe meant I was the one who had to carry the hurt and pain alone."

Ms. Jones leans in a bit. "That's a big secret to hold and carry alone. Did you find a way to process any of what came up?"

I pause, thinking. "Umm… I don't think I really knew how. That week, during a class change at school, I suddenly started crying uncontrollably. I remember wishing I could disappear. Then a friend asked what was wrong, and we sat outside. I unloaded everything. I told her what happened. At least as much as I could remember."

Ms. Jones nods gently. "How did it feel to finally not carry that weight alone anymore?"

"It made the situation feel more real, but at the same time, it felt good to talk about what happened."

"Was your friend able to show you the empathy you needed?"

"Yes. She just sat, listened, and hugged me. She told me she was sorry that I had to go through something like that. She is someone very special to me, and I don't think she even knows that."

"It sounds like that was a person you finally expressed trust in."

"Yeah, I guess so. I guess I had people in my life ready to be there for me, but I struggled to see it then."

Part Seven: Shifting Mirrors

"Were there any other friends you felt close to?" Ms. Jones asks.

"During that time of my life, there was another friend who was important to me but in a different way."

"Why is that?"

"Well, Tiffany was new to the school, hell, she was new to the country. Her family had just moved here for business. We had lockers next to each other in eighth grade, and she always struggled with her combination, so I'd help her open it. That's how we became friends.

She was bossy, but I liked how confident she was. We spent almost every weekend together, and during the school week, we'd stay on the phone for hours.

One day, we were dancing in her room, and she touched my butt and said, 'You have a great ass.'

It caught me off guard. I felt all these emotions at once, even new ones that made me question myself. When we'd lie down to sleep, she'd ask me to rub her back to help her fall asleep.

There was this one winter she stayed the night, and it snowed. I woke her up to look out the window, and she'd never seen snow before. Her face lit up, and something about her smile in that moment made me feel like I wanted more than friendship. It was pure. Soft. She looked so happy, and it made me happy just to witness it.

She asked if we could go outside and touch it. I warned her it was cold, but she didn't care.

We threw on shoes and ran outside in our pajamas. She grabbed a handful of snow, looked at me, and yelled, 'Holy shit, it's fuckin' cold!' I laughed and said, 'I told you!'

We had a lot of fun together. She was someone I eventually opened up to. I told her about my past; it took a while, but I did. And honestly... I think after that, I started to push her away." "Why did you push her away?" Ms. Jones asks.

"I think... because now she knew who I really was. And that scared me. I thought it would be easier to distance myself by hanging out less and risk being seen too deeply. And honestly... I was also struggling with wanting to be more than just her friend."

"What do you mean by that?" Ms. Jones asks, but I'm pretty sure she knew exactly what I meant.

"I had a crush on her. Seeing her face light up like it did that night made me want to be the reason she smiled like that all the time... but not just as a friend. I wanted her to be my girlfriend. I knew it probably sounded silly back then, but it was a feeling I'd never had before. I had a crush on my friend. And my friend is a girl."

"Did you ever tell her how you felt?"

"No way! I didn't even understand why I was feeling that way in the first place."

I pause, thinking back.

"I remember sometimes pretending I was a boy. I'd imagine how I'd ask girls out... like writing a love note or giving them a flower. I'd picture myself doing the things I wished someone would do for me, thoughtful, sweet stuff. It wasn't about being an actual boy. I think it was more about wanting to be the one who made a girl feel special, but to do that, I had to reassign gender roles. I didn't have the

29

language for it at the time that I was curious or a lesbian… so I kept it all in. Just silly daydreams I'd have when no one was around."

"Those are not silly thoughts. Are you two still friends?"

"No, we lost touch after I changed schools in 10th grade. We would talk on the phone here and there, but then it slowly stopped. To be honest, I think it was hard pretending and listening to her talk about the boy crushes she had when I wished she were my girlfriend. I felt like I opened up to her, and now I couldn't have her. Although I didn't tell her about my crush on her."

"Did you try to reach out to her after?"

"I asked some mutual friends about her, but that was it. It hurt too much."

"How was high school after that?"

"When I changed schools in 10th grade and went back to my old neighborhood. That's when I became 'the light-skinned girl' now. Girls always made comments that made me feel not enough. I was no longer the joke of being the white girl, but now the light-skinned girl that girls claimed I wanted their boyfriends. What's funny is I'd rather have them not the boy. But it was a lot." I say smiling.

Ms. Jones smiles back, a little caught off guard by my comment. "Did you meet anyone at the new school?"

"There was a boy, Rico. He became my first real boyfriend and was in 11th grade, a grade above me. He was biracial like me, which made me feel I could relate to him. We used to talk about having a family one day. We did not have much time alone because of his living situation and because we lived in different neighborhoods. He was my first real kiss, and it happened at a youth event. Kind of a funny story."

"A church youth event?" Ms. Jones asks for clarification.

"No, he was in a group home, and they were having a small event for them. I guess more so, just a get-together at one of the owners' houses with food, games, and stuff like that."

"He was your first boyfriend and first kiss. I'm sure that kiss is a good memory, and funny as you say."

"Yes… It was. And one I haven't thought about in a long time." I smile at the memory.

"My mom dropped me off, and Rico greeted me at the door with a dozen red roses. We walked down to the finished basement where the get-together was happening. We sat on the couch and turned on the TV. I was so nervous, he kept scooting closer and closer. Then suddenly, his arm was around my shoulders. I remember feeling sweaty and thinking, Great, now I stink.

Then he leaned in to kiss me… but I softly whispered, 'You just ate chicken wings.'"

Ms. Jones chuckles. "What did he say to that?"

"He jumped up off the couch and said, 'Okay, I'll go rinse my mouth real quick.'

As soon as he left the room, I started fanning my shirt to dry off and checking my armpits for sweat stains. I also puckered my lips and put on some Chapstick because this was it. This was the kiss.

My stomach was full of butterflies, and nervousness was taking over, but I had to play it cool. The door opened, and Rico came back smiling like he was ready for a movie scene. He sat down, put his arm back around me, and said, 'I'm ready now.'

And I was trying to stay calm, but part of me kept thinking, what if I mess this up? Then I got grossed out thinking about his spit in my mouth, so I had to mentally refocus again. And then… he kissed me. When we pulled back, he looked at me and said, 'Wow, you're a really good kisser.' I had no idea what I was doing," I say, giggling, "but apparently I did okay."

"I was nervous. But I liked him. Thought I loved him."

Reflection

Poetry was the first way I could express myself and my big feelings at such a young age.

Silent Goodbye

A silent goodbye. We both know we have to go.

There is nothing more to say or do. It is just time to walk away.

To go silently apart.

To no longer see each other as friends but as strangers.

A silent goodbye. I will cry a few tears for you, and I am sure you will for me.

I will always keep you in my thoughts.

But times have changed, and the world is going by.

We have to say our last goodbye silently.

You walk past me and I'll walk past you.

Part Eight: All I Wanted Was To Be Loved

Ms. Jones smiles. "That does sound like an important moment to remember. It was your first real kiss. Do you think you two were in love, teenage love?"

I nod thoughtfully. "For what I understood love to be at the time... yes, I'd say we were."

I pause, a small smile forming as I recall the moment in the present time. "It was sweet how it happened. One day at school, Rico asked if he could talk to me in private. I said, 'Yes,' and we walked to an empty classroom and sat down.

He looked me in the eyes and said, 'Do you know the difference between being in love and love?' I wasn't sure how to answer; I'd never even thought about that before. So, I just said, 'No... what's the difference?'

He started explaining that he'd talked to his counselor about it. And while he was talking, his eyes started to tear up. Then he said, 'Being in love is a feeling so deep that it consumes your thoughts and makes you want to be better.' He paused, took a breath, and gently touched my hand. Then he said, 'I'm in love with you... and I want to be a better man.'

I exhaled softly, remembering the warmth of that moment. "I hugged him. And it felt like we stayed in that hug for hours."

Ms. Jones speaks gently. "Those were big feelings to express at such a young age. How long did you two stay in a relationship?" I take a breath as if I were pulled back to that moment and those feelings. "Yes, it was a lot. And once he told me I had his heart, I wanted to do everything I could to protect it, to make sure we had a future together." I pause, with a sweet memory slowly turning.

"But just a couple of weeks later, a friend told me that Rico had been talking to other girls online. When I asked him about it, he denied it, saying they were just friends. At first, I wanted to believe him. But I started noticing him talking to different girls, acting like it was no big deal. Every time I brought it up, he reassured me 'They're just friends. Don't worry.'

Then one day, I walked up behind him while he was on the computer. I asked if I could read his messages from the little group chat he was in. He tried to talk me out of it, but I didn't back down. I read them anyway. He was telling other girls he didn't have a girlfriend. That's when I broke up with him. I walked away from him, so angry. He followed me, saying he was sorry, begging me not to leave him. But I didn't want to look like a fool anymore. I kept walking. I didn't realize it then, but that was the moment I started believing that loving someone meant being the one who got hurt."

Part Nine: Wish it Was Me

Ms. Jones shifts in her chair, "Was that your first heartbreak?"

"No... I wouldn't say he broke my heart just yet." I pause before continuing. "There was another guy at school I was close to named Jay. We'd talk on the phone for hours about everything. After the breakup with Rico, I vented a lot to Jay. He listened without judgment and told me I deserved better." I smile at the memory.

"He started leaving a single rose on my bookbag in the mornings. He'd walk me to class, carry my books, and would even write me love poems. He made me feel... seen and important."

"Was he your new boyfriend?" Ms. Jones asks gently.

"Not officially. We flirted a lot, but it wasn't a relationship. We even talked about me losing my virginity to him, though. He said he'd make it special with flowers, candles, and a mixtape he'd make himself. He made me feel safe. Like I could be myself." "Did you lose your virginity to him?" she asks with a smile.

I shake my head. "No, I didn't. But I've thought about it; if I had, maybe Rico and I wouldn't have been so back and forth. Maybe I would've let go sooner."

"Did you and Rico get back together and break up a lot?"

"Yes, we did. During one of our breakups, Rico asked to talk privately at school. We found a quiet spot, and he grabbed my hands.

'I want to tell you something before you hear it from anyone else,' he said.

"Right away, my stomach dropped. I could feel the sweat forming under my arms as I started to speak. 'Okay… what is it?' I asked.

"He looked me directly in the eyes and said it, just like that. He got another girl pregnant. I stood there, frozen, emotions flooding me all at once: shock, anger, sadness, confusion. 'Is she your girlfriend?' I asked him. Rico and I had started talking again recently, so I felt I needed to ask directly.

'No,' he said. 'I only love you.' Then he asked how I felt about it, and quickly said he wished the baby were mine. And the crazy part? I remember wishing that too. Even though I was too scared to have sex at the time, a part of me wanted a deeper connection with him, something that meant he was mine and only mine. He told me he still wanted to be with me. Then he asked, 'Would you take me back?' And I said yes. So just like that, we were back together."

"Were you okay with him having another girl pregnant?"

"No, but at that time, I loved him. At least I thought that was unconditional love. To be there by his side despite how I felt or how much it hurt."

"You were learning what love was to you, even if it meant putting how you felt on the back burner, but I hope you realize unconditional love doesn't mean accepting hurt. What came of you two?" Ms. Jones asked.

Reflection

Love is...

Love is something so hard to explain

Something you wish would always stay

How to say, "I love you."

And not have you run away.

How to say, "I need you." And not be too lame. Love is

the strangest thing.

so beautiful, yet so easy to lose.

Part Ten: The End of Innocence

"Well, at the end of the school year, Rico asked me to come to his graduation. He told me his biological father, who he'd recently reconnected with, was going to be there, and he wanted me to meet him."

"That sounds important," Ms. Jones replies.

"It felt like it. I begged my mom to take me, telling her I was his girlfriend and needed to be there to support him. I spent the rest of my money on him, getting him the perfect graduation gift. I made sure everything looked just right, down to the gift bag I put the gift in."

"That was thoughtful of you."

"Yeah… I wanted it to matter. The speaker that day was a social worker. She delivered a powerful speech about growing up in poverty and how your dreams are still possible if you pursue them. I remember sitting there, completely drawn in by her story. I even imagined myself being in her shoes someday, being able to empower others like she was doing for me in that moment." Ms. Jones nods, "That sounds like it made an impact."

"It really did. Then the ceremony started. They called names, and Jay's name was called first. As he walked across the stage, he looked over and winked at me. A few names later, they called Rico. He looked at me, too, and blew me a kiss. I blushed. I felt… chosen."

"They were both excited to see you, it sounds like. Did you get to see Rico after the ceremony?"

"That's where it all flipped. I rushed downstairs to find him and meet his dad. Jay stopped me at the door first. He hugged me and thanked me for coming to support him. I told him, 'Of course,' but I was already scanning the room for Rico."

"Still focused on seeing him."

"Exactly. Jay asked me to meet his mom, which I did out of respect, but I kept it short. Then I spotted Rico. I smiled... until I saw him. He was standing with his arm around a short, visibly pregnant girl, talking to a man I assumed was his father."

"Oh no," Ms. Jones replies, showing empathy.

"He looked right at me... and then looked away. Just kept talking like I didn't exist. I felt my heart sink. I felt so stupid. Jay called after me as I ran out, but I didn't stop. I found my mom and sister and told them I was ready to go."

"That must've been painful."

"It was. I spent the rest of the day in my room crying. Ignored everyone's calls, including Jay's. I only checked my phone, hoping Rico would call to explain and apologize... but he never did."

"Sounds like Jay was concerned and wanted to be there for you."

"Yeah. That night. He came to my house. He told me I deserved better than Rico, hugged me, and asked if I wanted to go out to a movie or grab food. I thanked him for checking on me, but I said I just wanted to be alone."

"That was kind of him."

"It was especially since it was his graduation night. Months later, Jay told me the baby wasn't even Rico's. All that pain I carried... and it wasn't even his baby."

Ms. Jones tilts her head slightly. "How did it feel when you found out the baby wasn't his?"

"Honestly, when I first heard the news, I felt happy. Almost relieved. But then, a wave of sadness hit me, thinking about how Rico must've felt. Even with everything, I still cared." I say, shaking my head. "It's strange how the heart works. How can you reach for the one who breaks it instead of the one who tries to hold it?

Looking back, I can see the pattern I fell into, loving from my wounds instead of my worth. I chose the familiar ache or the one who didn't show up while ignoring the one who did. I didn't have the language for it then, but now I can see it: I mistook chaos for love and effort for weakness. Jay was steady, gentle, and present while Rico was a storm. And somewhere inside me, storms felt like home."

"Sometimes we don't see what's right in front of us because we're still holding onto the hope of someone else," Ms. Jones says softly, jotting something down. "But the fact that you're able to recognize that pattern now… that's important. Awareness is the first step toward breaking a cycle." She pauses, giving me a moment to breathe into the truth of her words. Then gently, she asks, "Did you ever see Rico again after that?"

"Actually, yes. Not long after, I saw him standing at a bus stop. I was in the car with my mom. Our eyes met through the window. We didn't wave. We didn't speak. But in that moment... it felt like another silent goodbye in my life."

Ms. Jones nods gently. "Sometimes the most meaningful goodbyes are the ones we never speak. How was your relationship with your sister during this part of your life? You mentioned her a lot when talking about your early childhood."

"We didn't get along all the time. We used to fight constantly. But looking back, I think we were both just going through our own versions of pain and had no idea how to reach each other. I was a

41

depressed teenager, writing in my journal about wanting God just to take my life because I was so tired of feeling hurt. I'm sure she was hurting too... we didn't know how to say it to each other."

"Being a teenager is already a stressful time, especially when you're trying to figure out who you are," Ms. Jones said softly. "Did you ever think about hurting yourself during that period of depression?"

I nod slowly. "Yes... I think about it often. At times, it felt like I knew more about wanting to hurt myself than I did about how to live." I pause, swallowing hard. "The first time I tried, I was only seven. I was sitting in the bathtub and saw one of my mom's razors resting on the edge. I picked it up and cut my knee, then just sat there in the water... waiting. But I didn't really know what I was doing. I later realized that's not where people cut themselves to end life."

Ms. Jones' eyes softened. "Seven is so young to carry that kind of pain. Your comment sounds like that wasn't your only attempt. Were there more thoughts or moments like that as you got older?"

"I tried again in 10th grade," I admit quietly. "My friend was over at the time, downstairs watching TV with my sister. I wrote a goodbye letter because I felt so low, just completely numb inside.

I drank bleach, thinking it would finally end everything. But I didn't even do that right." I shake my head a little.

"All it gave me was an upset stomach and a pounding headache. I just wanted the pain to stop. I thought if I were gone, at least I wouldn't be hurting anymore." I pause, letting out a slow breath.

"After that attempt, I didn't try again as a teen. Something started to shift... life began to feel as if it were slowly changing for the better. I wasn't drowning in sadness like before."

Ms. Jones tilts her head, crossing her legs. "Changing how?" she asks gently.

"It was my senior year of high school, and I started at a new school," I begin.

"It was mostly white students, which isn't bad, but one of the first things I had to deal with was having a locker next to a girl whose grandfather was in the KKK. She thought it'd be funny to show me a photo of him in her locker." I shake my head. "Like it was supposed to intimidate me or something."

Ms. Jones raises an eyebrow. "Wow. Did it intimidate you?"

"No," I say, sitting up straighter. "I cussed her out. I had to let her know I wasn't the one. She didn't try that mess again."

She nods slowly. "I imagine that stirred up a lot for you. How was the rest of senior year at that school?"

"It was... okay," I say, with a slight shrug.

"I kept to myself mostly. Then my sister and I started hanging around with a few girls from school. We'd go over to one of their houses and make up dances together, just being goofy teens. That was probably the most fun I had that year, and it allowed me not to feel so down." I pause before continuing, eyes bouncing around the room.

"One of the girls, I started to feel really close to her. She was going through a lot at home,

and I was someone she confided in. I listened. We spent a lot of time together... and then,

just like before, I felt that feeling rise in me again. I started to have a crush on her."

Ms. Jones speaks softly. "Did you ever let her know about your feelings?"

"No, plus... I ended up meeting a boy who caught my attention around the same time. He was a good distraction."

"A distraction from liking a girl?"

I leaned back in my chair, caught a little off guard. I hadn't thought about it that way before. "I guess so."

Ms. Jones offers a warm smile. "You've shared so many meaningful pieces of your story today, and I truly appreciate how open you've been with me. Unfortunately, we've reached the end of our hour." She pauses before adding, "How about we start our next session with this boy and explore where that connection took you?"

"Okay, sounds good to me," I say, standing and reaching for my purse.

A small smile forms on my face. "I guess I really did open up today."

"You did," she says warmly. "And I hope we can keep moving forward like this. You're doing powerful work."

"Thank you," I say with a small smile. "See you next time."

As I walk to my car, my phone starts to ring. I glance at the screen and answer.

"Hello?"

"Hey, sister. How was therapy?" Linda asks.

"It was cool. Talked about a lot of my past… honestly shocked I even shared half that stuff with that lady."

"I'm really proud of you," she says. "I know it's not easy for you to open up about your personal life. But hey, Crystal called me. She said she needs to talk to you. Asked if you could give her a call if you're okay with it, I can text you her number."

I agreed, and we talked for a few more minutes before I hung up. But as soon as the call ended, a knot twisted in my stomach, unsure of what she wanted to discuss with me, considering I hadn't spoken to Crystal in years.

I stared at my phone, hesitating. Then finally… I dialed. The phone rang once. Twice. By the third ring, I was ready to hang up. But then she answered. "Hello?"

"Hey, it's me… Linda said you wanted me to call you," I said, trying to sound calm.

"Yes," Crystal said, her voice soft. "Thank you so much for calling. I just… I need to talk to you. And to tell you, I'm sorry."

Reflection

Why...

I sit and wonder why people say life is worth living and love is worth trying. Happiness is worth being, and sadness is worth leaving.

Then I say, why?

Why should I wake each day knowing I want to take it away?

Knowing love will never happen.

Happiness will never be, and sadness is a big part of me.

Now, please explain to me again why life is worth living.

Because you cry from joy, and I cry from pain?

Because you bought a new car and I, a new day?

You took the wrong street, and I can't find my way.

Life is worth living…

…when the pain fades away.

SESSION TWO

Part One: The Distraction

"Good to see you today. How was your week?" Ms. Jones asks as I step into the small, familiar office.

I sat down, exhaling slowly, debating whether to jump right into my week. "It was okay. After I left here, my sister called and said Crystal wanted to talk to me."

"Crystal, she's the older sister of your family friend, right?"

"Yes."

"Did you end up calling her back to find out what she wanted?" "I did." I pause for a moment, unsure if I want to go further.

Ms. Jones gently picks up her notepad. "Would you like to talk about how that conversation went?"

"Well, she answered and thanked me for calling because she needed to apologize to me. She went on to explain that she has been in therapy and working through her past. As I listened, she told me she was sorry for molesting me as a child. She went on to tell me that I was 4 years old when she forced herself on me and that she did not stop, even though I cried. She just kept talking about her life and how hard it has been to live with this secret and how she needed to talk to me so she could heal."

"That certainly opens a new door of emotions for you, I can imagine. How did it feel hearing her apologize?"

"I was shocked… and honestly, I'm still trying to process it." I pause, shaking my head slightly. "I never expected her to be the one to call. And definitely not to ask for forgiveness." Ms. Jones waits patiently, giving me space.

"I told her I didn't even remember it being her. I always remembered it being Frank. She said she had a feeling he was hurting me, too."

My voice tightens. "The worst part? It felt like the whole reason she called was to make herself feel better. Like saying sorry was some relief for her. Not for me. It wasn't about my healing; it was about the release of the guilt she felt."

I take a breath, steadying my voice. "I didn't want to forgive her. Every part of me said don't. But I said yes anyway. Not because I meant it… But because I knew she needed to hear it. And I didn't want to carry her pain and my own. I don't want to be the reason she doesn't heal."

Ms. Jones gently tilts her head, her eyes soft. "That's a heavy weight to hold. And a complex mix of emotions. I appreciate you sharing it. Do you want to share more of what you're feeling?"

I nod slowly. "It's just… a lot. Honestly, I don't want to sit with that today. Where did we leave off last time?"

"We'll go at your pace," she says calmly. "Last time, you were telling me about meeting a boy during your senior year. Would you like to pick up there?"

"Oh yeah, the distraction! I went to get my senior pictures taken, and after my mom, Linda, and I grabbed dinner. As we were in line at the chicken place, a guy behind the counter took our order. He kept smiling at me, and I could feel myself blushing because I wasn't used to that type of attention. Once we received our food, I made sure to sit where I could still peek at him. When we finished eating, we got up and walked to the car. I was getting in when he ran out yelling, 'Excuse me, can I please talk to you for just a minute?' I was so excited and so nervous because my mom gave me a disappointed look, but I told him, 'Yes.' He asked for my name and said he couldn't let me walk away without asking. He asked for my phone number, and I gave it to him. Once I got back in the car, my mother yelled at me for being disrespectful. I did not understand why she was so mad, so I tried to explain that he was sweet. She was not trying to listen. I tried listening to her, but my mind drifted to a guy named Keith. We spoke on the phone frequently, and it didn't take long for us to grow close. We had a lot in common. I told him I had enlisted in the Army, and he informed me that he had plans to join the Navy after he graduated."

"Was Keith someone who made you feel happy?"

"At that time, he made me feel special. He'd bring me little gifts, just because he was thinking of me. A few weeks before my 18th birthday, he surprised me with a CD I had been wanting. I played it the moment he gave it to me, dancing around my room with excitement."

I paused, a soft memory forming behind my eyes.

"As I was dancing, he pulled me close and kissed me. One thing led to another, and he gently laid me down on the bed. All I could think was, Oh shit, this is really about to happen. He pulled out a condom while I slid off my pants. We kept kissing… and then it happened." I allow a small smile, remembering that moment, "I kept my eyes shut tight the whole time, until he stopped and asked, 'You okay? Do you need me to stop?' I opened my eyes and told him, 'No.' I shockingly felt safe. It didn't feel rushed or forced. It just… happened."

Ms. Jones nods, listening closely.

"Afterward, he went to the bathroom to flush the condom, then came back and asked how I was feeling. I told him I was okay. But then he said, 'Good… but we might have a problem.'"

"I looked at him and asked what kind of problem. That's when he told me the condom broke."

"Wow," Ms. Jones murmurs.

"Thankfully, I ended up starting my cycle a couple of weeks later. But waiting for my period. That was pure panic."

"That had to be a scare for you both. How was your relationship with Keith after that? " Ms. Jones asks.

"Honestly, he started getting needy. He wanted to be around me all the time," I say, shifting in my seat. "A few weeks later, I broke up with him."

Part Two: Clingy Love

"What led to that decision to break up with Keith?"

"The idea of pregnancy shook me. It made me realize I wasn't ready for something that serious. We still talked after that and stayed friends for a little while, but I didn't want to be in a relationship with him anymore." I pause, then continue. "Around that time, I started talking to other guys, too. I figured I was still young, not locked into anything serious, so there was nothing wrong with exploring."

Ms. Jones nods, encouraging me to keep going.

"But Keith didn't take it well. He started getting down about us being just friends. He didn't want to be left out of anything. He'd ask me to come with him to parties, to the movies...anywhere I was going with my friends. I felt bad for him, so sometimes I'd let him tag along."

I pause again before adding, "And Jay was still in the picture, too. He'd been consistent the whole time, and he even bought me a ring because he said he wanted to marry me."

"It sounds like guilt may have kept Keith around longer than you intended. Also, wow for Jay, did he get down and propose with the ring?"

"No. I never saw the ring. He told me I could see it if I said 'yes,' but I never felt the same way. I tried... really hard, but I couldn't be with him other than as friends."

"Sounds like you were in a bit of a love triangle. Both guys wanted something serious with you, but you were still figuring out who you wanted. How did that feel for you?"

I take a breath. "Honestly… I think I liked feeling wanted, for once. I had gotten so used to feeling alone, like no one really saw me. So having two people show up and want me… it felt good, as bad as that might sound."

I pause, fidgeting with my fingers before I add, "But if I picked just one, I was afraid the other attention would disappear. It's like… I wanted the comfort and attention of both. Like I wished I could combine them into one person, the perfect partner."

"Yes," Ms. Jones says with a soft chuckle. "I understand that feeling very well. Wanting to build your ideal partner. Do you think, back then, or even now, that one person wasn't able to give you the attention you needed?"

I tilt my head, thinking for a moment. "Now that you put it that way… yeah, I guess I did feel that way. It always seemed like the moment you commit to someone, they get too comfortable. Like… they stop trying and pull back." I pause, then add, "People change once there's a label on the relationship. But even with all that, I still ended up saying yes to Keith again. He was just so persistent, he really wanted to be my boyfriend, and I gave in."

"How was the relationship with Keith the second time?"

"Okay, I guess. We spent a lot of time together and grew close. I even opened up and shared my past with him about Frank."

I take a deep breath. "I trusted him a lot. I shared how I was scared to walk by myself because I feared being raped. So, he started picking me up from school as often as he could. My classmates would even come to find me and say, 'Your boyfriend is outside.' To add, Keith and I were having sex a lot. We had sex everywhere, all over town."

I giggle. "There were a few times we went to his place, and I would have to hide in the closet because his mom came home early. I knew she would have flipped if she had seen me there, but being a mom now, I understand."

"Now this sounds like teenage love." Ms. Jones says, smiling.

"Umm... I guess you could call it that. He was immature and needy, but I loved him," I say with a soft shrug. "We did have fun together. One of the sweetest things he ever did was send me on a scavenger hunt around the neighborhood."

Ms. Jones raises an eyebrow with interest. "Really? What was that like?"

"He created clues, and they were personal," I say, smiling at the memory. "Like, 'Go to the place where we sat for hours talking.' So, I went to this park bench we used to hang out on, and there was a single rose waiting for me, along with another clue."

"He had me driving all around, following these little notes with clues to the next location, and eventually, the last one led to an address with a room number, a motel. When I got there, he opened the door, smiled, and handed me a dozen red roses. It was sweet... and honestly, really romantic. Motels weren't so bad back then." I giggle while being caught in the memory.

Ms. Jones smiles gently. "That does sound like a lot of effort. It meant something to you."

"It did," I nod. "But... things started to change between us after that."

Part Three: When My Voice Went Silent

"What happened that changed it?"

"After I graduated from high school, I found out I was pregnant this time for real."

Ms. Jones gently leans forward. "What was your first reaction to the news?"

"I was shocked," I admit. "I didn't want to believe it at first. I just kept thinking, how am I going to tell anyone? What will they think? I didn't want to disappoint my family or my friends."

Ms. Jones nods. "Why did it feel like being pregnant would be a disappointment?"

"My life was already mapped out. I had everything planned, the dates, the deadlines, the dreams. I was supposed to leave for basic training just a few weeks after graduation. And then... I found out I was pregnant."

Ms. Jones leans in slightly, her tone soft. "How did that affect your plans?"

"I started questioning everything," I respond. "All the certainty I'd felt just vanished. I already felt a connection with the baby, but I also knew that if I kept it, nothing in my life would ever be the same. My mother strongly agreed. She told me flat-out that I had to have an abortion because she wasn't going to help me raise a child. She even said that if Keith didn't pay for it, she would."

I pause, swallowing back the lump forming in my throat. "That hurt. Hearing her say that if I kept the baby, I'd be on my own... it broke something in me. I felt powerless. Like... I could feel this life growing inside me, and I couldn't even protect it."

Ms. Jones nods gently. "That's a tough situation to be in, and I can understand why you would feel powerless. What was Keith's response to what was going on?"

"He wanted to keep the baby. He told his mom, and then she called me. Said she didn't believe in abortions and that she would take the baby herself, but she also mentioned raising the baby as she saw fit."

My voice tightens. "That made me so mad. Hearing her say she wanted my baby like it was something she could have. I told her, If I can't raise it, then no one will."

Ms. Jones meets my eyes, calm and steady. "Why do you think that upset you so much?"

"I think I was upset because my mother wanted nothing to do with my baby," I say, starting to feel the hurt from it again. "And I was scared... scared that she'd end up raising my child as her own. That I'd have to ask permission just to see my own baby. That idea haunted me. Then I realized I never even stopped to consider... maybe she was just trying to help. But at that moment, it didn't feel like love. It felt like control. It was just so much going on, and I really didn't have anyone to process with at that age."

Ms. Jones gives a small nod. "That's an understandable fear. When someone's love comes with conditions, it can feel like a trap more than support, especially when you didn't have the space to process everything." She pauses. "Do you know how Keith felt about the situation?"

"He cried to me a few nights before the scheduled abortion," I say softly, my eyes lowering. "Told me all he ever wanted was a family of his own... and that I was taking it from him. It upset me. The night before the procedure, I sat in my room, talking to the baby. I told her how sorry I was… and how selfish it would be to bring her into this world without the ability to give her what she deserves. I just knew she was a girl; I could feel it deep in my spirit, like a knowing or something. I just felt like I wasn't ready and upset at myself for being in that situation."

Ms. Jones gently asks, "That can happen when you are connected to the child. Honestly, Nadia, what you were doing takes courage; you were acknowledging your situation. Did Keith go with you to the clinic?"

"Yes, he came to the clinic after we arrived. When the nurse called my name, I followed her upstairs into this empty, white room. There was a hospital bed in the center of the room. She pointed to the corner of the room and told me to pick out a gown from a bin. I started digging through, searching for a purple one, my favorite color. I finally found a light purple gown and put it on. I climbed onto the cold bed and lay down, staring at the ceiling, trying not to cry while I waited for the doctor to come introduce himself."

I pause for a moment before continuing. "I remember feeling so scared. So alone. The doctor came in and explained what would happen, and the nurse stood beside me, holding my hand. She gave me this warm, soft smile that brought a tiny bit of comfort… then told me to count backwards from twenty."

Ms. Jones stays quiet, giving me space as I continue.

"After the procedure, I woke up in a room with several other women who'd just gone through the same thing. I remember lying there wondering how they were feeling… if they regretted it as I did. Eventually, they told me I could get dressed and go downstairs. When I walked back into the waiting room, Keith, my mom, and Kristen were there. We all got in the car and drove home in complete silence."

"Thank you for sharing about that day, Nadia. I can only imagine what you were feeling that day. Was Keith supportive after the abortion?" Ms. Jones asked gently.

"Umm… he came to see me the next night," I said slowly. "We went for a ride because I needed to get out of the house to get some fresh air. We talked a little about basic training, the abortion… plans for our future. At first, it felt okay, like maybe we were finally on the same page."

I paused for a second and shifted in my seat before continuing.

"We ended up pulling into an empty school parking lot just to keep talking. He put the car in park, then unbuckled his seatbelt… and reached over to unbuckle mine, too. That's when his whole tone shifted."

Ms. Jones nodded slightly, staying quiet.

"He told me he was mad at me. Said I took away his chance to have a family. I told him I didn't have a choice… but he snapped, yelling that I could've given the baby to his mom."

I shift again in my seat. "I did not respond, then he leaned over trying to kiss me while lowering my seat. I told him calmly that I couldn't have sex until I healed and that I wanted to take a break from sex with everything that had just happened. He did not say anything; instead pressed his body on top of me. I raised my voice a little louder, asking him to please stop. I told him that I am still in pain from the abortion. He said, 'Maybe you deserve to be in pain.' I screamed, 'Get off me!' as he grabbed hold of my hands to pin them against the car window on the passenger side. I screamed 'stop' until I realized my voice was not being heard."

The silence filled the space between us. Ms. Jones nodded gently, her expression full of understanding.

"I'm so sorry that happened to you," she said softly.

"I don't think I realized at the time that it was rape," I whispered. "I thought… maybe I'd sent mixed signals somehow. That maybe I owed him something because of the abortion or because we were 'together.' But I said no. And I know he heard me. He just didn't care."

"What did you do?" Ms. Jones asked gently.

"I lay there," I said, my voice low. "The whole time… just lay there, while the tears rolled down my cheeks. I kept thinking, Did I deserve this? Was this payback for what I did?"

Ms. Jones didn't speak. She just listened, which somehow made it easier to keep going.

"When he finished, he pulled away as if nothing had happened. He didn't say much. Just drove me home and dropped me off like I was nothing."

I paused, staring at the floor for a moment.

"I walked into the house, got in the shower, and let the hot water run until it felt like it was burning my skin. I couldn't get clean. Then I went to bed and didn't say a word to anyone."

"To answer your question… no, he wasn't supportive about the abortion. He wasn't grieving the way I was. He was focused on getting revenge with me."

Ms. Jones's eyes softened. "Did you ever tell anyone what happened that night?"

I shook my head slowly. "No. Not a soul. I believed during that time that's what I deserved."

Ms. Jones's eyes soften. She sets her notepad down slowly.

"I need you to hear me clearly," she says, her voice firm but gentle. "No one deserves to be raped. Not ever. What happened in that parking lot was not your fault. 'No' always means no, whether whispered, shouted, or said through tears. That was not love. That was a violation of your body and your trust."

She pauses, letting the words settle.

"You've been carrying that for a long time… silently." Then she gently continues, "You did nothing to deserve being raped."

I take a deep breath, "I kept things to myself so no one would feel like they had to deal with my problems."

Ms. Jones nods slowly, her expression full of empathy.

"I'm glad you're able to speak about this now. You have shown such strength in one lifetime, and I'm grateful you are sharing your experiences with me. Did you continue to have contact with Keith after he raped you?"

Eyes fixed on the floor as I processed what Ms. Jones said to me before letting out a small breath.

"I lost so much of myself that day. The pieces I thought I had control over were taken… forcefully. Again."

My voice hesitates, but I keep going.

"I stayed with him because… I felt guilty. I had taken away the family he wanted so badly, and I carried that guilt like it was mine to hold."

I pause, pressing my palms against my knees.

Part Four: The Day an Angel Found Me

"A month later, we both shipped out for basic training on the same day. The first thing we do is meet with a doctor to make sure we are physically ready for training. During the medical processing, one of the doctors asked me if I had ever had a miscarriage, a live birth, or an abortion. I answered yes to the abortion. He asked for the date, and when I told him it was recent, he followed up by asking whether I'd had a normal cycle since then. I told him no. That's when he told me I couldn't ship out until I'd had three regular periods."

"What happened next?" Ms. Jones asks.

"He sent me to speak with someone about changing my ship-out date and returning home until then. As I waited to meet with the scheduling sergeant, something inside me snapped. I felt like I couldn't take one more disappointment. I planned to go into the bathroom and unalive myself. I figured I could use my shoelaces to tie on the exposed pipes.

I walked into the bathroom to scope it out. But as I stood there, other girls walked in. I froze. I turned around and walked out, sitting in one of the chairs directly across from the bathroom, just watching the door... waiting for them to leave." My voice cracks. "The sadness drained out of me, and what was left was anger. I felt angry at everyone, at everything. I just kept telling myself I was done."

"Since we're sitting here together now, I take it you didn't follow through with that plan. What helped change your mind that day?"

"The scheduling sergeant called my name before I made it back to the bathroom. As I took a seat across from her, she looked at me and asked, 'What's going on?' in such a concerned way. And just like that, I lost it. I cried and poured my entire life story out in that little office. For two hours, I told her everything, how my dreams had shifted again, how I felt like I was always starting over. I told her about Frank and how he messed up my life. She just listened as I used her as my human journal.

Once I took a moment to breathe, she stood up, walked around her desk, and hugged me. That moment... I didn't have to earn her care. She didn't want anything from me, just to be there. She encouraged me not to give up. Said she believed I had a reason to be on this earth. She even shared parts of her own story, and that helped me see I wasn't alone." I pause, my voice is softer now.

"I really believe she was an angel. Not the kind with wings, the kind sent to step into your life at the exact second you need a reminder. That day gave me a flicker of hope that maybe other women out there had been through what I had and survived. That maybe I could too."

"Did you ever see her again?" Ms. Jones asks.

I shake my head. "No. I never saw her again after that day."

I paused, glancing down at my hands. "But sometimes I wonder if she was even real. Like maybe... she was an angel. Not a wings-and-halo kind of angel, but something deeper. A soul sent to catch me before I fell too far because I survived that day because of her."

Ms. Jones leans in slightly. "You believe she may have been a spiritual guide or something like that?"

I nod slowly. "Yeah. I never shared that story with anyone before, but the way she showed up just when I was ready to give up felt too perfect to be a coincidence. And the way she hugged me... it didn't feel like just a hug. It felt like something... more."

Ms. Jones gives a soft smile. "Sometimes we don't recognize divine intervention until we look back. I'm glad you were seen and comforted that day."

"Me too," I whisper. "It made me realize maybe I'm not as alone as I always thought. Maybe... someone up there is still watching out for me and sees me." I say, shrugging my shoulders. "When I returned home, I did write her a letter and bought a card, but I had no address to send it, so I held on to it to remember that day."

Part Five: What It Means to Be a Woman

"How were things once you returned home?"

"It was okay, I guess. I had a lot of emotions just sitting at home while Keith shipped out. It felt unfair; he still got to move forward with his life, his goals, while I was left behind to carry the weight of everything."

"Did you feel he should have been sent home, too?"

"I felt like everything about it was unfair. I had to wait three months to ship out, and I didn't even have a choice when it came to keeping my baby. That Keith could rape me as punishment and still walk away without a single consequence. Yeah... it was unfair his life didn't stop or even slow down for something we both went through."

I pause, then add, "Guess that was my first lesson in what it means to be a woman."

"What do you mean by that 'lesson in being a woman'?"

"I mean… life has a way of being cruel to women," I say slowly, the words heavy on my tongue. "It tells us to be strong, to endure, to carry everyone else's weight and never drop our own. We're expected to bleed quietly, cry discreetly, and keep going like nothing ever happened. And somehow, we're still supposed to have dinner on the stove, the house clean, and a smile on our face like we're not breaking inside." I pause; eyes fixed to the floor.

"It's like we're punished for feeling. For remembering. For being soft. For not being soft enough. And when we break… no one shows up to help put the pieces back. We learn how to walk around shattered."

Ms. Jones nods gently, her tone softening. "That's a powerful statement. Do you feel like life has been unfair to you?" I let out a tired breath.

"I do. But I also feel like I don't even have the right to say that out loud. Because there's always someone who's had it worse. Someone who got hit harder, silenced longer, hurt deeper. So, I silence myself to protect others from my truth." I glanced out the window. "But deep down, yeah… I do feel like life's been unfair. And some days, I wonder if I was born to carry pain that wasn't mine."

"I think life is unfair to many people. But for women, especially the ones who've been hurt, we seem to have the smallest voice. People slap labels on us as 'angry,' 'difficult,' or 'bitter,' but we have things to be angry about. And honestly? That's okay, I feel." I exhale sharply. "Anyway… back to being sent home, right?"

Ms. Jones nods. "Okay, but this is your space, so you lead, and I will follow."

"Thanks," I say with a quick smile. "During my time back home, I was watching TV when the news cut in, showing the second plane crashing into the Twin Towers. I just sat there, frozen, watching the world unravel on live TV. I couldn't believe what I was seeing. I called Keith's mom to see if she had heard from him, but she hadn't. That's when I started to worry that he was allowed to make a quick call every day, and I hadn't heard from him. I know I shouldn't have cared, not after everything, but that's always been my weakness… caring for people, even when they don't deserve it." I pause, swallowing hard.

"He finally called about forty-eight hours later. He said security was extremely tight, and they weren't allowed to make any calls. When

9/11 happened… after everything else I'd just been through… that was the moment I felt myself slipping again. I think that's when depression hit me full force."

"What makes you say it was depression?"

"I couldn't get out of bed most days. Nothing felt worth doing. I didn't want to laugh, didn't want to be around anyone, and listening to music wasn't comforting. Eating felt like a chore. I'd pick at food and then push it away. I was just… numb. I slept more than usual, but never really felt rested. It reminded me of how I felt as a teenager… only now, I finally had a name for the sadness."

Ms. Jones nods softly. "You're describing depression. Do you remember if you were able to do anything to help yourself feel a little better?"

"My high school friend Kristen and I decided to spend some time together before I left. Honestly, during that time, I was just ready to ship out."

"Did you have to wait long before you were able to ship out?"

"I shipped out in October, which was three months after my original date. It wasn't long, but it did feel like I waited forever."

"Once you made it back, did you see the Angel Sergeant who spoke with you before?" Ms. Jones says with a warm smile. "I looked for her… but no, I never saw her again."

"Do you think going back to basic training felt like an escape for you?"

"Yes. It was. I needed something to focus on, something that forced me to keep moving, to stop thinking about my life."

Part Six: Wearing Masks That Silenced Me

"How was training once you were able to return?"

"It was a lot. They broke me down in ways I didn't even know I could be broken. I quickly grew stressed and waited for the mail, hoping people were missing me. I struggled a lot during basic, to be honest, both mentally and physically. My legs were in pain all the time, and it was hard for me to do physical training. But I met some interesting people. We were able to be there for each other and grow a bond."

"Are you still in contact with some of those people?"

"Just one person, but we do not see each other as often as we would like because we live in different states. But we stay in contact."

Ms. Jones leaned forward slightly. "With everything you've shared, do you see anything that might be affecting your situation today?"

I looked down, picking at my fingernails. "I don't know... I guess it felt like I didn't have many people who truly understood me. And the ones who did... I either pushed them away or they eventually left. Maybe some people cared, but back then, it didn't feel that way. Granted, there were some people there, I guess. I don't know."

She nodded gently. "That's one way to look at it. Another might be to ask: did you build walls so high that no one could reach you, even if they tried?"

"People always let me down," I said softly. "Why would I fully let them in?"

Ms. Jones's voice was calm. "Were you afraid to let people in?"

I paused, then looked up. "I was afraid to let myself in."

She shifted gently in her chair, curiosity in her eyes. "What do you mean by that?"

I exhaled slowly, searching for the words. "I wore so many masks, Ms. Jones... I became whoever people needed me to be, so that I wouldn't be a burden. I smiled when I was breaking. I laughed as I screamed inside. I made myself small so others could feel big around me. I wasn't a bad kid; I did what I was told, respected adults, and followed the rules, but I never felt like anyone really saw me. I didn't just wear masks to protect myself... I wore them so well, I didn't know who I was."

My voice cracked, but I kept going. "I didn't know how to say, 'I'm hurting,' or 'I'm scared.' I thought if I told the truth, I'd be pushed away or punished... or worse, ignored. So, I kept everything in. Still do, sometimes. Because if I let myself feel it all, the pain, the loneliness, the anger...I'm scared it would swallow me whole. I think I feel too much... and I never knew what to do with all of it."

Ms. Jones nods, her voice gentle but steady. "People often wear many masks to survive, especially when the world doesn't give them space to be their full selves. Those masks aren't weaknesses; they're often our armor. But armor gets heavy. And it can start to feel like the mask is all there is." She leans in slightly, her tone inviting. "I think exploring your past is helping us peel some of those layers back so we can find the parts of you that were always there, even under all that weight. Those parts are still longing to be seen. I want to continue there, if you're ready. What happened between you and Keith after basic training was complete?"

"Well, the day of my graduation, my mom, dad, and Keith came to see me."

Ms. Jones tilts her head slightly. "Your dad was there?"

"Yes. He was kind of in and out of my life growing up, but before I left for basic training, I reached out and told him. He said he was proud of me. Actually... everyone was proud of me, or at least that's how it seemed. They all came down for graduation, and it felt good to have both of my parents there in the same place, celebrating me as cheesy as that might sound."

I pause, a faint smile crossing my face. "We all drove home together. It was a little awkward, but also... I don't know, nice."

Ms. Jones smiles. "That sounds like a meaningful moment, and nothing wrong with a little cheesiness in life sometimes. After graduation, were you stationed somewhere else or back in your hometown?"

"I was in the National Guard, so we stayed in our home state unless activated, and I say we, meaning Keith and I. Once I got back home, things between Keith and me felt... different." Ms. Jones leans in slightly. "How were they different?"

"Well, Kristen and I had already made plans to get a place together once I finished training. But then Keith called one day, saying he was getting kicked out of his parents' house. He told me we needed to hurry and find an apartment together."

I sigh. "I told him I wasn't ready for that. I even suggested he stay with some of his friends. But he kept pushing, saying none of them could help. He made it sound like I was his only option." Ms. Jones watches me closely, but says nothing, giving me space.

"I gave in. We found a place within a couple of weeks and moved in. But if I'm being honest... I think he knew I had saved most of my basic training money while he had blown through his. Part of me felt like he needed me financially more than anything."

I pause, eyes drifting back to the floor. "Or maybe... maybe he just didn't want me out of his sight. The control was subtle at first, but it was there. And even with all those thoughts racing through my mind,

I still agreed to move in with him. I think a part of me hoped that if I could just be what he needed, he would finally see me in the way I'd always been waiting for… for someone to see."

"You don't sound happy about living together and can't help but wonder if this was out of guilt." Ms. Jones observes gently. "Were you two officially in a relationship at that time, or still just friends?"

"We were in a relationship," I reply quietly.

She gives a slight nod, then glances at the clock.

"It looks like our time is up for today. I'd like us to continue exploring your relationship with Keith in our next session; there's still more to unpack about what happened. Do you already have your next appointment scheduled, or do you need to set one up?"

"I have one," I say, standing slowly and grabbing my purse. "Thank you, and see you next week."

As I walk toward the door, I feel the weight of everything we uncovered still lingering in the air, but also… a small breath of relief.

Session Three

Part One: The Breaking Point

My phone started ringing just as I was pulling into the parking lot. I debated answering, but when I finally said hello, I heard her on the other end.

"Can you please talk to me?" Dasia's voice cracked at the other end. I could already hear that she's been crying.

I closed my eyes, jaw tight. "I don't have anything to say to you."

"Please. Please just let me explain what happened…"

"I saw what happened, Dasia!" I snapped. "So no, there's nothing more to say!"

"It wasn't what it looked like, baby. I swear. Just give me a chance to talk to you. Please don't shut me out again. I would never intentionally hurt you."

I hated that she still called me baby. Like the word could undo what I saw. Like it could erase the betrayal that was burned into my chest. I also hated not knowing the whole story, but either way, I saw the text messages, and I can't be looped into the drama… I'm tired.

"I said no." My voice came out low and cold.

She was quiet for a second… then her tone turned sharp. "So, this is it then? Are you just going to throw us away? You aren't even trying to hear me."

"There's nothing left to hold onto," I whispered.

Dasia paused, breathing harder than usual. "Fuck it. You're so damn stubborn! Nothing is ever good enough for you. All you do is push people away the minute they disappoint you. I'm trying my hardest to love you."

I swallowed hard, gripping the steering wheel. "If you say so," I muttered. "I'm busy and don't have time for this right now." I didn't wait for her to reply. I hung up.

The silence afterward hit harder than the call itself. I dropped the phone into the cup holder and took a sip of water, but it didn't soothe the burn in my throat. I sat still, staring out the windshield, blinking back the tears that gathered. Ugh, this stupid therapy is not helping shit at all! I shouted, slamming the water bottle into the seat next to me. You can't love me and hide shit… how is that my fault? I opened the car door and stepped out into the heavy air, walking toward the building with my heart pounding against my ribs. I signed in quickly, not even looking at the receptionist.

Before I could sit down, she called out, "You can go ahead and walk back. Ms. Jones is ready for you."

Great. No time to pull myself together. I walked down the hall, pushed the door open, and stepped into Ms. Jones's office.

She glanced up from her paperwork with a warm smile. "Hello, Nadia. How has your week been?"

"It's fine," I snap… settling into the dark brown couch with a heavy sigh.

Ms. Jones glances up. "Are you sure?"

I narrow my eyes. "Why? Am I answering that wrong, too?"

"You aren't answering wrong. I'm questioning because something in your tone tells me you're not being honest with yourself or me." She gently sets her papers aside.

I cross my arms, heat rising in my chest. "Look, I came here to figure out my life right now. But all we've done is dig up my past. That's over. I don't see how it matters anymore. It's the present that's got me all fucked up."

Ms. Jones leans forward slightly. "What I hear is frustration. Maybe even anger toward this process. Is that fair to say?"

"Yeah. That's exactly it," I mutter. "I'm pissed. And I'm tired of circling shit that already happened."

"Learning about your past helps me understand who you are today," Ms. Jones says gently before opening her folder again. "Once we explore those early relationships, we may uncover some patterns that shed light on your current situation."

I shrug. "I guess."

Ms. Jones looks up from her folder, sensing the tension. "Before we jump back in… do you want to talk about what's going on right now? You seem like something's weighing on you."

I cross my arms. "I said I'm fine."

She nods slowly, not pushing. "Okay. Just know this space is yours, you don't have to carry it alone if you don't want to."

I shift uncomfortably. "I just want to talk about what we were talking about before."

"Alright. We can pick up where we left off. You mentioned living with Keith once you both got back from the training."

"Oh… yeah," I say, trying to pull myself together. "Well, Keith and I had our first apartment together. I had plans to start at the local college a few months after moving in. He went with me to the college orientation. I was so excited about it, but Keith was so negative. He kept saying it wasn't fair for me to start college when he couldn't. I told him he could fill out a college application, but he said he didn't want me around all those guys at school. He wanted me to wait until he could start so he could 'make sure I was okay.'"

"Did Keith fill out a school application?"

"No, we started working. Well, he started working, and I sat at home. He felt that right now wasn't a good time to start college. He also decided that I owe him a family. My job was now to get pregnant while he went to work, which led to us fighting a lot. I guess we were both angry, just for different reasons."

Part Two: Held Hostage By Guilt

"Fight how?" Ms. Jones asks, her voice steady but gentle.

I lean back, letting the weight of the memory settle in my chest.

"Over everything. Over nothing. If I wanted to go out, it was a fight. If I didn't want to have sex, it was a fight. And he knew just what to say to make me feel like I was the problem."

Ms. Jones tilts her head slightly. "Did you feel like you were the problem?"

I nod slowly. "Yeah. I started to believe it. Like maybe I was being selfish for not wanting what he wanted… or for wanting more than just being someone's girlfriend or baby mama." I pause, staring off toward the floor.

"It was just so much fighting and yelling all the time," I say, my voice dropping. "I felt like I was always walking on eggshells. Then… I started talking to Jay again. I told him how unhappy I was, how trapped I felt, but I also told him I didn't know how to leave. I had spent all my money and had nothing outside of Keith."

I exhale slowly, the memory still stinging.

"One night, I went over to his house just to hang out, and… we ended up having sex for the first time."

Ms. Jones's expression stays calm and open. "With Jay?"

"Yes, Jay. A couple of weeks later, Jay showed up at Keith's and my apartment late one night wanting to talk. Jay really was a good guy and thought he was saving me." I smile for a second before it fades.

"That's when the truth came out. Keith found out I had cheated. I blurted it out because I thought that would finally be the end. I wanted him to leave me, man, I wanted it so bad. I thought if I made him so upset with me, then he'd want to break up for sure, and I would figure out how to live again, but... he didn't."

Ms. Jones tilts her head gently. "Once Keith heard about the cheating... what happened?"

"Jay and Keith just started yelling at each other," I say, my voice flat with the memory. "I stood in the hallway with Jay, hoping Keith would say, 'Go on and leave with him.' But instead, he just yelled at me to go back inside. And I did. I was so mad at myself for not having the guts to walk out that door. I felt like a prisoner with invisible bars." I pause, swallowing hard.

"That night, Keith lost it. He screamed at me, saying, 'If you leave me, I'll kill myself.' Then he grabbed a knife and started cutting his arm. Blood splashed onto the white hallway walls of the 2-bedroom apartment. He repeatedly yelled that I couldn't leave him and that it would be my fault if he died."

Ms. Jones speaks gently, trying to keep her expressions professional. "What did you do while he was yelling?"

"I stood there," I whisper, "feeling ashamed saying it out loud. I was frozen. Watching him bleed and yell while basically falling apart." I blink; eyes focused on a small plant on Ms. Jones' desk. "When he stopped cutting, he raised his arm and punched the wall right next to my head. I flinched. Turned and saw the hole his fist left behind. I remember standing there... wishing I could disappear."

"How did his behavior make you feel?"

"I was scared that I would go to jail if he killed himself. I started to feel trapped. I felt I couldn't tell anyone, so I stayed. I stopped talking to anyone, just stayed in the house, and waited for him to come home from work. A few weeks later, I took a pregnancy test since my period was late."

Reflection

My Strange Lover...

We sleep as if we are strangers in bed; you lie your way, as I lie mine.

How soft my caress is against my own skin.

How safe my body feels gathered in the pillows that hug me tight.

No love is shown as we sleep through the night.

No arms to wake up in or forehead kisses, for I am east, and you are west.

We are worlds away in the same bed.

Two bodies that remain two bodies throughout the night.

Waking from a bad dream to find you nowhere in sight

...just the lifeless pillows that never left my side.

Only empty smiles as I wake, for you were north and I was south.

Two bodies, one bed, with no fairy tale end.

Part Three: A Hot Dog After 'I Do'

"What did the test say?"

I looked directly at Ms. Jones as I answered her question, "I was pregnant. And I didn't even know how to feel about it." I looked down, resting my hands in my lap. "I didn't know who the father was because there was a chance it could have been Jay. I told Keith I was pregnant, and he got excited… and all I could do was stare out the window, hoping he wasn't the father."

Ms. Jones stayed quiet, allowing the weight of my words to sit in the space between us.

"I wasn't excited like most women are when they find out. I didn't feel joy; I felt like the air had been sucked out of the room. I wasn't working. I wasn't in school. I wasn't doing anything with my life but sitting in that apartment, waiting for Keith to go to work so I could breathe and wait for him to come home so I wouldn't feel so alone. As well as waiting to get pregnant for him. Most women experience postpartum after the baby is born… but mine started the moment I saw that positive test. That was the moment I realized I might never experience life the way I dreamed."

"Did you share these feelings with anyone?"

I shook my head. "I didn't have anyone to tell. I didn't talk to my friends much anymore because every time I got on the phone, Keith was right there, sitting next to me, listening. If I wanted to go out, he wanted to come too. He said it was because he loved me, but I started to feel like I couldn't breathe without asking permission. So, I stayed in the house… and little by little, I let Keith become my everything."

Ms. Jones leaned forward, her voice gentle. "It sounds like there were a lot of emotions tied to that relationship; more pain than peace. Did things get any better while you were pregnant?"

"Things calmed down a little between Keith and me once he found out I was pregnant. He was excited, like, really excited, to have what he called 'his family finally.' We found a new place and started settling in. It felt… okay for a while."

I paused, then added, "My unit ended up getting sent overseas, but they discharged me because now I was pregnant and couldn't go with them."

Ms. Jones made a small nod. "How did your family take the news of your pregnancy, or did you let them know?"

"Keith's mom was over the moon. She kept saying she hoped for a granddaughter. I told her I'd see what I could do." I chuckled lightly, but the smile faded quickly. "My grandmother, on the other hand, asked if we were planning to get married. I mean… I grew up Southern Baptist, and in our church, having a baby out of wedlock was frowned upon. So, about a month before my due date, we went to the courthouse to get married.

"Did you want to marry Keith?" Ms. Jones asked gently, her voice careful not to press too hard.

I look down at my hands, picking at chipped nail polish on my thumb. "I wanted peace," I say finally. "I wanted the noise to stop. The questions, the judgment, the expectations. Marrying him felt like... the right thing to do. Or at least, the thing that would shut everyone up."

Ms. Jones watches me closely. "That's not the same as wanting to marry someone."

I nod slowly. "I know. I didn't marry him because I was in love. I married him because I felt like I had to. My family expected it, his family expected it, and part of me thought maybe if I just followed the script, things would finally feel stable."

"Did things feel stable after?" she asks.

"No." I let out a small, bitter laugh. "I remember standing in that courthouse, wearing this simple dress shirt that barely fit over my belly. I should've been excited. But all I kept thinking was... this isn't my story. This isn't how I imagined my life."

Ms. Jones leans forward slightly. "What was your story supposed to look like?"

I shrug, eyes burning, holding back tears waiting to be released. "Freedom. Purpose. Joy, maybe. I don't know... just something that didn't feel like settling. Or like I was just surviving. I loved the idea of marriage more than who I was marrying," I admit, my voice soft with reflection. "While we sat on the bench outside the courthouse before seeing the judge, I looked at him and asked if this was really what he wanted. He shrugged and said, 'Yeah, I guess. What about you?' I said the same thing. We both agreed to something neither of us seemed certain about."

I pause, shaking my head lightly. "We went inside with my mom, my sister, and his sister. We said our vows, exchanged rings, and came out husband and wife. There was no celebration, no dinner, no reception, no honeymoon. Just me, standing outside the courthouse in a wrinkled dress shirt with my pregnant belly peeking out, getting a hot dog from a street cart." I paused and glanced down at my phone, buzzing in my hand, to silence it. "That was our beginning. And even then, that hot dog tasted more like an ending than a beginning."

Part Four: I Didn't Want Him. I Wanted Me

"How were things between you two after the marriage? Was there still abuse in the home?"

I shrug, silencing my phone again. "Umm... I don't know... not that great."

Ms. Jones watches me, giving me space. "Is everything okay?"

"Yes, just turning my phone down."

She nods, but her eyes don't miss the shift. "How were things once you had the baby?"

"Our son decided to come around two in the morning. I woke Keith up, and we rushed to the hospital. I remember being nervous, but there was also this strange calm that came over me. It was like everything around me just paused for a moment, and all that existed was me and this little life about to arrive. Holding him... that part was magical. I mean, I was scared, terrified even, but I was also in awe.

This tiny person looked up at me like I was his whole world, and I didn't even feel like I knew how to be in my own world yet, but there he was... needing me to figure it out. The next night at the hospital, Keith said he had to leave for work, leaving me alone in the room. It was quiet, almost too calm. And I realized, for the first time, I was entirely responsible for someone else. I had never even changed a diaper before. I just stared at my son, and he stared back like he already trusted me. That realization made me cry. No one else came to visit that day, so it was just the two of us. A brand-new baby and a woman trying to figure out who she was."

"Did you ever find out who the father was? I know you mentioned being unsure."

"He looked like Keith, the good parts of him so… there was no question. He was the father." I answer quickly, almost like the words sting a little.

Ms. Jones tilts her head gently. "During this time, did you have an outlet, something like a hobby, journaling, or even someone to talk to in your family? You were going through a lot emotionally… a new baby, an abusive marriage, and your unhappiness."

I shake my head. "No, not really. I didn't have the energy for hobbies. And talking to family meant being honest. That wasn't an option. I didn't want to hear the 'you chose this' lectures or feel like a burden. I just kept everything inside, tried to survive one day at a time."

She gives me a moment, not rushing the silence.

"Honestly," I continue, "I was disappearing inside myself, and no one even noticed. I barely understood what was happening, and I was living it."

"Plus, he didn't like me leaving the house, so I stayed home, unless we all went out together. He liked knowing I was home, taking care of our son. Then he picked up a second job because we needed the money, even though I suggested getting a job myself to help."

"Keith was the sole provider?" Ms. Jones asks, her pen gliding quietly across the notepad. "Did you like staying home?"

I shrug. "It was okay, I guess. But being in the house all the time started to feel like a slow death. I'd get bored out of my mind. We had two cars, but I never had any money to go anywhere. It was like I had the freedom to move but nowhere to go and no one to be." I paused, staring past her for a moment. "One day, I was home, bored, and decided to look through our cell phone bill. Just something to do, really. But then I saw two new numbers. He was calling them a lot, and always during the times he was supposed to be at work."

"Uh-oh, what did you do?" Ms. Jones asks as she stops writing.

"I called them," I say flatly. "Both numbers. And both times... women answered."

Her brows lift just slightly. "Did you confront him about the calls?"

"Hell yeah," I say, glancing down at my phone. "If he was cheating, I was ready to leave. That was going to be my way out. I asked him about it when he got home."

"What did he say?" Ms. Jones asks.

"He said they were just women he met at the gas station. I asked him flat-out if he was cheating, and he said they were only his friends. Then he flipped it and got all mad, talking about how he's allowed to have friends. I told him, yeah, sure, everyone's allowed to have friends... but why were his only friends women, and why was he only calling them during his third shift at work?"

Ms. Jones raises an eyebrow. "Were you allowed to have male friends?"

I scoff. "I wasn't allowed to have friends, period. I asked him, 'Would you like to get a divorce so you're free to do whatever you want?' He told me, 'No, you're not taking my family away from me again.' I pause before continuing. "The next day, I got my son and me dressed and went to the gas station just to see who these 'friends' were. As soon as I walked in, I looked at the cashier's name tag. He had already given me their names, so I was looking to match faces."

"Were both of them working that day?"

"No, just one of them," I reply. "I walked up to the counter, and she greeted me all polite. I didn't waste time; I asked if she knew Keith. She looked a little nervous and said, 'Yes.'"

I glance down at my hands, then back at Ms. Jones. "I told her I was his wife, and that we had a son. Then I asked her straight out what was going on. She told me she had a feeling he was married, said he came in one day wearing a ring, and then stopped wearing it. She said she even asked him if he was married, and he told her not anymore." I smirk, letting out a soft laugh. "I said, 'Oh, I'm surprised he would lie.' But she didn't laugh at my little joke. She just looked kinda uncomfortable. Told me she was sorry and that he was always coming in asking to hang out, but she never went anywhere with him. Said something didn't feel right."

"And how did you respond to that?" Ms. Jones asks.

"I told her it was okay… and next time he comes in, just let him know you talked to his wife." I pause, chuckling again. "I walked out of that gas station like I was confident."

Ms. Jones nods. "That was big of you to handle it directly and calmly. How did you feel after?"

"Honestly? I felt powerful. Not because I wanted him because I didn't but because I finally took back some of my respect. It wasn't about love; it was about reminding myself I still mattered. I guess giving myself love."

Ms. Jones' voice softens. "That's a big shift. Did you confront the other woman, too?"

Part Five: The Other Woman

"The other woman worked third shift, so I called her cell during the day since I had her number. I didn't come at her with anger. I just wanted to know what she knew. I told her Keith has a wife and a child. She sounded more confused than rude. She told me Keith had promised her they would be together one day, that he'd even met her son, and they'd all spent time together like a little family.

It was honestly comical. I know I should've been mad, but it was hard to be angry at someone who sounded so lost. She wasn't trying to be disrespectful. She didn't know. I told her, 'You should probably stop talking to him.' She said, 'I'll try.'

A couple of days later, she called again. Told me that Keith was still calling her. He told her we were separated and that I'm lying about being married. At that point, I was done explaining and started getting irritated. I said, 'Believe what you want. I told you the truth.'

The fact that she was now questioning me like I was the liar, that's when I went straight to Keith. I asked him directly what was going on. Of course, he flipped the story and claimed she kept calling him, that she wanted him to play daddy for her son. I asked, 'Did you two have sex?' He said, 'No, but she gave me head... twice.' I stood there, silent for a second. Then I told him, 'Change your number, now!' Which he agreed and did.

Looking back, I don't know what hurt more, the lie, the truth, or how calm I had to stay through all of it. I started to wonder if love was supposed to feel like confusion, even when it remained silent. Suppose being a good partner meant swallowing my hurt to keep the peace. But deep down… I was tired, but we had a child together, so I had to keep going."

Ms. Jones nodded, her expression softening. "That's a heavy burden to carry alone, feeling like love means holding your breath, or making yourself smaller just to avoid more pain. That kind of silence can start to feel like survival." She paused for a moment. "It sounds like they were telling you two different stories. How did that make you feel, knowing someone was lying to you?"

"I went back and forth about who to believe," I admitted. "I was confused about how to even feel because I wanted to leave Keith, but I also started to feel… hurt. Not even just mad. But it hurt.

To make matters worse, his best friend had moved into the same complex as us. So now, after work, Keith would hang out over there, sometimes for hours, before even coming home. His best friend had a serious girlfriend. At least that's what I was told. One day, while doing laundry, I found movie tickets in Keith's pants pocket. I asked him about it, and he said he and his friend went to the movies. 'To see a chick flick?' I asked. Then he said, 'Well, my boy's girl went too, and she picked out the movie.' So, I asked, 'Why didn't you invite me?' He told me, 'Because someone had to watch our son.'

I wanted to believe that. I really did. I accepted the answer and walked away… but something didn't feel right. There were only two tickets. His friend's girlfriend was supposedly there, so where was the third ticket? I silently asked myself. I couldn't let it go.

So, I checked the phone bill. Even after changing his number, he was still calling that woman."

Ms. Jones leaned forward slightly. "He didn't stop talking to the woman?"

I shake my head. "No. And that's when I realized he never intended to."

Part Six: The Silence of My Anger

"I planned to find out if they were still in contact," I continued. "I called her and asked if she was still talking to Keith. She said, 'Yes,' and told me he still came over to play with her son on his days off. Then I asked her about the movie. She said he had taken her on two double dates with his best friend. Said Keith told her we didn't live together anymore, that he changed his number because I kept calling him." I paused for a moment, clenching my hands in my lap, remembering how low it made me feel back then. "I wanted to scream. But then she said, again, 'I'm sorry. You seem like a nice person. I'll talk to him about what's going on.' That's when I started to question everything. Why did she need to talk to my husband about what was going on between us?

The pain of his cheating didn't even hit me first; it was the anger. Anger that she was getting the softness I had been craving. He gave her what I'd been needing from him and was giving this other child attention when he had his own at home."

Ms. Jones' voice remained steady. "Did you talk to Keith about what you were feeling?"

"Yes. I confronted him that night. We argued loudly. I told him he was a liar. Instead of answering me, he deflected. He started yelling at me about Frank and what happened when I was a child. He screamed, 'You didn't tell anybody because you liked what he was doing.' Then he shoved me into the bathroom. I ended up

on the floor, got up, feeling cornered, and I jumped into the bathtub. I sat in the tub with my hands over my ears. He stood over me, repeating, 'Admit you liked it. Admit it.' I screamed at him to stop before he finally walked away."

Ms. Jones exhaled gently, her eyes never leaving mine. "He took the heat off himself and tried to weaponize your past. That is not just deflection, that's emotional abuse. He was trying to mentally harm you by reopening old wounds that were never his to touch. I'm so sorry you had to endure that, especially on top of everything else. What happened between you two after that?"

"We continued like we always did," I said, "Just... functioning. Going through the motions. He stopped working his second job, but nothing felt any different. I felt so numb and was just going through the routine of being alive, not actually living. There was a time my friend Kristen called: she'd gotten into a physical fight with her boyfriend and asked if I could come get her. Keith overheard and said he was coming with me. I told him I was fine to go alone, but he insisted. So we all went and picked Kristen up. We got her and started driving her back to her mom's. Keith drove, my friend in the passenger seat, and I in the back with our son."

Ms. Jones nodded slowly, listening as I continued.

"On the way there, we started arguing again, about her, the woman he was still talking to. My anger just boiled over. I grabbed his wallet and tossed it out the window. Right there on the highway."

Ms. Jones raised an eyebrow gently. "Why did you toss his wallet out?"

"I felt like... if he didn't have his license, then maybe he couldn't leave. Maybe he'd stop disappearing and leaving me to just sit home and babysit our son like I didn't matter. I was angry. I was tired of him deciding everything. It was silly, I know."

I looked down at my hands. "He then yelled at me. Called me a 'bitch.' My friend snapped at him, told him not to talk to me like that. I yelled at him too… and then I smacked him on the side of his face."

"In the car?" Ms. Jones asked softly. "While you were in the back seat?"

I nodded. "Yeah. I just… reached over and smacked him. It wasn't a planned reaction; it sort of just happened."

Part Seven: Breaking Point

Ms. Jones gives a soft nod. "How did Keith respond?"

"When we pulled up at my friend's place, he reached into the back seat and started squeezing my temples. I tried to push his hands away, to wiggle free, but he just kept squeezing tighter. Our son was in my lap, crying, watching it all unfold."

Ms. Jones leaned in. "He grabbed you while you were holding your son?"

"Yes," I say, shaking my head. "I finally got my head out of his grip… but then he wrapped his hands around my neck. Tight. He looked me straight in the eyes as he squeezed. My entire body started getting hot. I remember tasting something… like burnt rubber in my mouth. My vision blurred. I felt like my eyes were about to pop out of my head. That wasn't the first time he attempted to physically hurt me, but it was the first time he tried to choke me."

I swallowed hard. "And then… I heard my son cry. It pierced through everything. My friend was screaming at him to get off me. I shouted and motioned at her as I started fighting out of his grip again, 'Take him! Take my son upstairs!' She didn't want to leave me; she kept saying 'no,' but I forced the baby into her arms and told her to go. She finally ran."

"I grabbed my phone, the diaper bag, and my wallet, although all I had was a few dollars in there. I tried to get out of the car, but

90

as soon as I put one foot down, he jumped out and grabbed me and threw me to the ground. Then he picked up my wallet, took the money, and snatched my phone."

I could feel my heart pounding again, just recalling it. "I tried to run toward the apartment, but he grabbed my legs and flipped me onto my back. I kicked and screamed, fighting him off. That's when he started biting me, biting my body like an animal." Ms. Jones' face softened with pain.

I pause as my mind drifts back. My voice softened. "A woman was walking past on the sidewalk. She saw us. I know she saw me because we made eye contact for a moment. I screamed out, 'Help me, please! Call the police!' But she didn't stop. She just shook her head and hurried away."

Ms. Jones leaned in, her tone gentle but tight with concern. "She didn't stop to help?"

I shook my head slowly. "No… she didn't. I could tell she was scared. I was mad then, and I didn't fully understand it. But I get it now. Sometimes women are afraid to intervene for fear of becoming a victim, too. It's sad, isn't it? That we live in a world where helping someone could get you hurt. So instead, we walk away."

"You're right," Ms. Jones said, her voice low. "It is terrifying to consider stepping into danger, even when our hearts want to help. It's the weight women carry… being expected to save others while fearing we won't be saved ourselves. Being a hero can become the victim." Ms. Jones says, looking down at her notepad before glancing back up to ask. "What happened next? How did things work out for you in that moment?"

"Well… we went at it a little longer outside until I was finally able to run inside the apartment. While I was running up the steps, he grabbed my leg, causing me to fall, attempting to drag me down the steps. I kicked him hard, where the sun doesn't shine, as they say, and ran into the house where Kristen and my baby were. We slammed the door and locked it behind us to keep him out." Her eyes widened slightly as I continued.

"My friend had called the police. So when they got there, they took pictures of me. I was covered in bruises and bite marks. They suggested I go to the hospital. So, my mom came to pick me up, and we drove to the ER.

I remember sitting on that hospital bed, hoping they'd give me something for the pain. The nurse came in and said the doctor wanted X-rays, so they drew some blood and handed me a cup to pee in. When I came back to the room, I sat on the edge of the bed, exhausted, hurting, just waiting to be done. The nurse walked in, holding my chart close to her chest, and said it like it was nothing: 'Your pregnancy test is positive.' Then she walked out. Just like that.

I sat there, stunned... wishing I could disappear. Like if I sat still enough, I'd evaporate into the air and leave that hospital gown behind."

Part Eight: Wanting To Vanish

Ms. Jones kept her voice soft. "That is some news to hear in the emergency room. How did you feel after hearing that you were pregnant?"

My voice broke slightly. "To be honest, the world just... stopped. Everything in me shut down. I didn't want to cry. I didn't want to scream. I didn't want to breathe. I just wanted to vanish. It felt unfair, painfully unfair. After everything he'd just done... now I was pregnant by him again? I felt trapped. He had just beaten me, and now I was carrying his child again."

"Did you tell him you were pregnant when you found out?" Ms. Jones asked gently.

"Not right away," I said, my voice low. "He was picked up on domestic violence charges and taken to jail. And when they arrested him... he still had the apartment keys in his pocket."

I let out a bitter chuckle, but there was no humor in it. "So, I was locked out of my own home the entire weekend. I couldn't even get in. No clothes, no crib, nothing."

Ms. Jones tilted her head slightly. "What did you do?"

"That Monday, I scraped together what I could. My mom gave me what she could in cash, and I rented a car from this low-budget place down the road. I remember the seatbelt didn't click right, and the check engine light was on. But I just needed to get to the rental office. It literally was like a bootleg car rental place." I respond with a small giggle.

"I've heard about those a few years ago but wasn't sure if they were real. Guess you answered that for me." Ms. Jones says with a soft smile. "Did they let you into your apartment?"

"They told me there was a fee for a new key, but I explained I didn't have the money, which was so embarrassing for me, plus I had to show the police report. They agreed to unlock the door and said to let them know when I left so they could secure it again." I swallowed hard. "Once inside, I just... snapped. Anger took over. I grabbed some clothes and then broke down. I started crying, hitting myself in the stomach. Then I grabbed a bottle of pills and swallowed a handful, hoping I'd miscarry. I didn't want to bring another child into this. Not into this life. Not with him. I felt this baby deserved better than what I could offer. I hated that I kept being in that situation, and I hated even more that I didn't know how to fully get myself out of it."

I looked down, feeling guilty for speaking that out loud. "I loaded my son in the car and drove back to another friend's house. Or at least... I think I did. Everything went blank after I stopped at the rental office. The next thing I remember was waking up, parked in front of another friend's place. I believe my guardian angel came back and drove us there. Because I have no memory of that drive. I know I took too many pills and regret it to this day for ever doing that."

"What did you do when you got there?" Ms. Jones asked, her voice steady but sounding concerned.

"I asked my friend to help me get my son out of the car. Then I went inside and slept for hours. Just... disappeared into sleep." "Do you remember how you felt after taking those pills? And what were you hoping would happen?" she asked softly.

I shook my head. "I don't remember feeling anything except numb and sleeping. I just didn't think bringing a baby into that situation was fair. Not for me. Not for the baby. I didn't want another child by him. He wasn't a good man. He wasn't safe." I looked down at my phone before asking, "How much time do we have left?"

Ms. Jones glanced at the clock. "About fifteen minutes."

"Okay... can we stop here for today? I need to go," I said, already standing.

"Of course. I hope everything is okay."

"It's fine. Thank you." Sounding uneasy and impatient.

Reflection

Silently...

Shh... No one speaks; this argument is carried out in a silent way.

You walk past me as I walk past you,

Now let's pretend we're not under the same roof.

How loud the words are that aren't even shouted.

How intense the push is without even feeling it.

Nothing's getting solved this way,

Yet I won't be the first one to break.

Don't walk into the same room as me because it is getting hard...

...not to look at your face.

Don't lie in the same bed as me, for you might wake up in my personal space.

You did me wrong, yet you believe the opposite, and now we are stuck in this silence as if neither one of us exists.

This is bull if you ask me, yet I don't want to be the first one to break.

Instead of saying 'sorry,' you'd rather have this argument in silently. Shh...

Session 4

Part One: Guilt-Laced Love

"I'm sorry about last week," I say, stepping into the room. "I was just going through a few things and needed to get out of here. I guess talking about my past, while trying to manage everything going on in my life right now... is overwhelming. Maybe this therapy stuff isn't meant for me."

Ms. Jones nodded with calm understanding. "That's okay. It's your choice whether you continue or need a break. Therapy is not meant to push you past your limits; it's meant to open the door to healing. With each session, I'm learning more about who you are to the world and to yourself. As well as who you are becoming."

I shifted in my seat. "What does that mean, Ms. Jones? Am I crazy or something? Be honest. I can totally take it if you think I am too dramatic or crazy."

She met my gaze directly. "No, not at all. What I mean is... I hear you telling me a story, but it's as if the emotion has been stripped away. You're speaking as if it happened to someone else. That's not craziness. That's survival. But healing requires more than surviving. It means letting yourself feel what you once had to numb and not running or separating yourself from it."

I looked away, shrugging. "Everyone's been through something. Everyone has a story. Mine just happens to suck. And I don't like talking about it, never have. But if sitting through these sessions is what I need to do to prove I'm okay, then fine. Let's keep walking down memory lane, I guess."

"I want you to know," Ms. Jones said, her voice steady and warm, "that you do not have to prove anything to me. I'm not here to judge you or evaluate your worth. I'm here to help you sort through your emotions, no matter how tangled they feel. This is your safe space."

I sank into the chair and nodded, feeling the knot in my throat tighten. "Honestly, I don't even know how to feel about anything right now. Some days I wake up numb. Other days, I'm angry and don't even know who to be mad at. There are rare days I find reasons to smile again."

I take a pause. "I left off last session when Keith was in jail, right?" I say, trying to pull myself back into therapy.

"Yes, but before we start back, do you want to explore the emotions you are feeling now?" Ms. Jones replied softly.

"No, I'm okay, let's just keep moving forward. So, he stayed locked up for about a week... until our first wedding anniversary." I let out a small breath. "I bailed him out that day. I thought maybe it could be a fresh start. They say the first year of marriage is the hardest, right? I figured... maybe if we could survive that, we could survive anything."

Ms. Jones leaned in slightly. "Did you want things to work out between you two?"

"I don't know," I admitted, my voice barely above a whisper. "I just knew I was about to be a young mother with two kids. I was scared. Terrified to do it alone. So yeah... I wanted it to work. I needed it too. And maybe part of me still believed he could change."

I looked down at my hands, twisting my fingers. "But there was another part of me that felt... guilty. Guilty for putting my husband

and the father of my children in jail. Guilty for messing up his record, his future. Guilty for being the one to tell. And I kept wondering, what if he hated me now? What if I made it worse?"

Ms. Jones nodded slowly, letting the weight of my words settle. "That's a heavy load to carry, Nadia. And I want you to know, it's not uncommon for survivors to feel guilt, even when they've done nothing wrong. Especially when love and trauma have been so tightly woven together. But hear me clearly: you didn't put him in jail. His actions did. And your fear... your guilt... those are wounds, not flaws."

I swallowed hard as I listened.

She continued gently, "It's okay to have wanted love and safety and connection. And it's okay to have hoped he'd become the man and father you needed. That doesn't make you weak. That makes you human."

"Being a human sucks," I said sarcastically, trying to mask the ache in my chest with a weak smile.

Ms. Jones let out a soft laugh, her eyes kind. "Yes... I agree. It really does, sometimes."

There was a pause, a softness in the air that made it feel safe to be real and honest.

"What are you thinking, Nadia?" she asked gently.

"Yes. At the time, I did," I admitted. "I get it now, that was on him. He made the choices. He had control over his actions." I paused. "Not that I was totally innocent either, I know I was angry and said things and smacked him, but he attacked me. He tried to kill me. So... he did that to himself. And acted that way in front of our son."

Ms. Jones nodded slowly. "All actions have a reaction."

"I agree," I said quietly, but with certainty.

"What happened after you bailed him out?"

I let out a long sigh. "When he got out, he came straight to my friend's house, where I was staying. Like, didn't even hesitate. Showed up to let me know he was out and wanted to talk. I don't know what I expected, but part of me was relieved he didn't come back angry."

Ms. Jones waited, listening.

"We went home together," I continued. "And he said he wanted to fix things. That he wanted to work on our marriage, really try. We agreed not to give up. We even talked about going to counseling together. It felt... hopeful. Like maybe we could reset."

I paused, my throat tightening again. "But even in that moment, a part of me was wondering if I was forcing hope where there wasn't any."

Part Two: False Starts

You both agreed to try marriage counseling? That's a big step. Were you two able to work together and grow from it?"

"Well... not really. We ended up doing marriage counseling through his Pastor at the church he grew up in. From the start, I stayed mostly silent. Keith painted the whole situation as if everything was my fault. When the Pastor asked if there had been any infidelity, Keith immediately said, 'No.' I just sat there, quiet, listening to him lie while the pastor congratulated us for being faithful."

I paused before continuing, "I barely spoke during that session; Keith took over most of the answers. We set another appointment, but I knew I wasn't going back."

"Why didn't you want to continue?" Ms. Jones asked gently.

"What was the point of going if we weren't working on the real issues? Keith told me he didn't want everyone in our business. He believed what happened in our household should stay there. I asked why we were even in therapy if we weren't going to be honest. He told me it was because he said we could go, like he decided to allow it.

In our second session, he tried again to answer all the questions himself, but the pastor interrupted, saying he wanted to hear from me. I froze. I wasn't sure what I was allowed to say.

Then the Pastor asked me directly if there had been any infidelity. My stomach twisted. I didn't want to lie to a Pastor in church, but I also didn't want to fight with Keith. I told the truth. I said, 'Yes.' Keith looked at me like I had betrayed him.

When the Pastor asked who, I opened my mouth, but Keith cut me off, saying it was my fault he cheated. The pastor calmly told him that no one else controls our choices, that Keith was responsible for his actions. He told him he was the man of the house and needed to protect his family. To protect his wife, both physically and emotionally, while putting God first.

I hoped Keith was listening. I expected something would shift. But on the way home, he didn't speak to me. Hours later, he exploded. Said I had disobeyed him. That I had no right to tell our business, he yelled, 'I'm the man of the house!' so he totally took what the Pastor said out of context and created his own meaning."

Ms. Jones asked, "Did you two continue to seek therapy?"

"No," I replied. "That was the end of that. He told his Pastor we had worked through everything and didn't need to come back. But things were far from fine between us."

I shifted in my seat. "At the time, Keith was still awaiting trial to determine if he would be charged with domestic violence. When we went to court, they told me that if I reduced the charges to a disturbance, he'd be allowed to stay in the military and deploy overseas, since his unit had recently been activated. I debated it and decided to drop the charges… and he was charged with disturbing the peace."

Part Three: The Shitty End of the Deal

Ms. Jones asked gently, "Was Keith staying in the home with you after he got out of jail?"

I shook my head. "Not really. We were barely speaking. We fought all the time, so he stayed over at his friend's house most nights."

"Was he helping you with your son during this time?"

"No, not really. He didn't provide or support me as a parent. He'd occasionally ask to see the baby. But even that came with drama."

"How was it drama?"

"One day, he said he missed our son and asked if he could spend a few hours with him. I agreed. I walked him around the corner to his friend's place. When Keith opened the door, I stepped inside and instantly smelled smoke. There were liquor bottles all over the table. It wasn't a place I felt safe leaving my baby."

I paused, my voice dropping low. "Sometimes it feels like my whole life has just been one fuck up after another. Every time I try to do better, I end up in the same damn cycle, just a different day, but the same pain. Like, healing keeps getting postponed or isn't meant for me."

Ms. Jones leaned in just slightly, her voice soft but steady. "I want you to hear something clearly: what you experienced isn't your fault. Surviving isn't a failure. You were doing your best with what you had. Honestly, you handled things better than I would have given your age. You were in your early 20s, I assume."

I looked down at my hands. "I was 20 years old, actually. It just always felt like I was drowning, and no one saw me. Like I was screaming from inside a glass room and people just kept walking by."

Ms. Jones nodded gently. "That's a very real feeling. And now… you're finally being heard. I'm listening to you."

I let a deep breath out as I felt my eyes starting to water. I glanced at my phone, pretending to check the time but really just trying to hold myself together.

She asked softly, "How did he respond when you said you didn't feel safe leaving your son there?"

I swallowed. "He pushed me away from him and started laughing, saying he was fine. I told him not to push me because I was pregnant. He laughed harder and shoved me into the wall, saying I was lying."

Her face shifted slightly, her brows pulling together, but she said nothing.

"I reached for my son again and told him I wasn't leaving the baby there. He pushed me over the back of the couch, and I rolled down to the floor. I felt so helpless. He's 5'11, and I'm 5'4, so I was nothing more than a rag doll. I screamed at him to stop, reminding him again that I was pregnant."

I paused, feeling heat rise in my cheeks as if it had just happened. "And he kept laughing. Holding our baby in his arms, laughing. He looked at me and said, 'You're only saying that, so you don't lose me."

Ms. Jones blinked slowly, her voice calm but sure. "That's manipulation at its worst."

"Yeah? I stood up and told him, 'Trust me, I don't want you." "You

stood up for yourself in that moment," she said gently.

"Yeah, but that made him mad, so he pushed me again. I'd get up, and he'd push me right back down. I finally crawled away so I could stand up. I ran to the diaper bag, pulled out the doctor's paperwork, and told him, 'It's in writing.' He smacked the papers to the ground and told me it wasn't his baby.

I picked up the papers and said, 'Just give me the baby so we can leave.' When I told him that, something in him snapped. He pushed me away and laughed while I tried to stand. I kept telling him I was pregnant. I kept reaching for my baby. Nothing stopped him. He shoved me again and again, until I was on the floor, dizzy and shaking, and he was still holding our child, still laughing. Then I screamed at his friend to tell Keith to stop. The whole time, the guy had just stood there, watching. Finally, he said something and told Keith to chill out. I got up and went outside to call the police.

When the officer arrived, I told him what happened and tried to show him the bruises. But the cop told me that, since Keith was the father, he had a right to see his son. I yelled, telling him Keith had been pushing me, hurting me. I showed him my arms. He looked me in the eyes and said, 'If you don't calm down, I'm going to have to take you to jail.' He walked over and talked to Keith. A few minutes later, Keith handed the baby over to the officer and said he had somewhere to be."

Ms. Jones blinked slowly, absorbing every word. "Again, I am sorry you experienced that, but you were determined not to leave without your son. You are a strong mother. How did it feel... knowing he didn't believe you were pregnant?"

"He knew I was pregnant," I said quietly. "I don't know why he had to be such an ass about it. Maybe he didn't want to face the truth, but it made me not want to have another child by him. I felt humiliated. Hurt. To hear him laugh at me... and then call me a liar, like I made it all up to trap him, not to mention a liar is such a pet peeve of mine."

I paused, my voice tightening. "And the worst part? He did all of that while holding our son. Tossed me around like I was nothing... in front of our baby. That shame? That image? It burned. It's like I was chosen to get the shitty end of the deal in life."

Ms. Jones's voice was steady, but curious. "What do you mean when you say life gave you the shitty end of the deal?"

"I mean..." I shook my head slowly. "I've always tried to stay positive. I wanted to believe people were good deep down. Maybe if I loved enough, I'd get love back. But life just kept proving me wrong. Love didn't seem to exist, at least not the love I thought existed."

A bitter laugh came out. "People suck. How could someone... push me around like I was a stranger? Like, I was some side chick he barely cared about? That shit hurt. And I gave that man a whole son."

I looked down, my voice cracking just slightly. "I didn't want much. I just wanted to be loved. And feel safe. I just wanted to feel seen."

Part Four: Searching For God in the Hurt

"Is feeling safe with a person important to you? And what does safe look like for you?" Ms. Jones asked, her pen gliding softly across her notepad.

I nodded slightly, the words already forming in my chest. "Yeah... I guess it is. I feel like I spend so much time worrying about everyone else, making sure they're okay, but who's worrying about me, or just asking how my day is and meaning it, not just using it as small talk. When I say safe, it's just a space where I can be me and not have to hide my fears, flaws, or my goofy sense of humor. I paused, then added quietly, "So yes. I want to feel safe in a relationship." I paused again, glancing out the window.

Ms. Jones looked up and met my eyes. Do you believe in a higher power? Or practice any faith? I know when you were younger, you discussed going to church, but are you currently?"

I tilted my head slightly. "I consider myself a spiritual person. Why do you ask?"

"Because sometimes, having something, someone, bigger than us to hold onto helps us get through the hardest days. It gives us a reason to keep going when things feel too heavy to carry alone."

I nodded. "Yeah... I believe in God. I've prayed since I was a kid. Grew up in church. But I wouldn't say I'm religious, not in the traditional sense. I guess... I feel more spiritually connected, but I don't attend any particular church. Not sure if that's still considered a religion or something."

Ms. Jones smiled gently. "That's still faith. And that spiritual connection? It's been carrying you more than you realize."

"May I ask," Ms. Jones said gently, "do you see a difference between being religious and being spiritual?"

"I sometimes try to figure that out too, but my understanding of religion," I began, "is that it's more about strict beliefs, like following one system and rejecting all others. Honestly, sometimes it feels like a cult with too many rules. Spirituality, to me, is different. There are no rules."

"No rules?" she echoed, curious.

"Yes. No rules on how you believe. Like... I believe in God. But I also believe in things like reincarnation, that some people carry old souls. I could go on and on about it, but... maybe we should stay focused before I start rambling," I said with a small laugh.

Ms. Jones smiled. "Maybe we can revisit that in a later session. I'd love to hear more if you're open to it. But let me ask... has being a spiritual person helped you get through your tough times?"

I exhaled. "I was more religious back then. And honestly? I struggled... a lot. My relationship with God felt strained when I was with Keith. He was so mean. I remember asking God constantly what I did wrong to deserve all that pain. I really thought I was being punished."

Her tone softened. "I don't believe it was punishment. No one, I mean no one, deserves abuse in any form as punishment for wanting to be loved."

"People say that," I muttered, my voice distant. "But why else would someone go through so much pain in one lifetime? Some would say karma from a past life... but I'm not sure I fully believe that."

Ms. Jones didn't rush to answer. She let the space breathe before speaking. "I wish I had the perfect answer for that. But I like to believe... sometimes the strongest souls go through the most pain so they can help guide the ones who feel too weak to survive theirs." She offered a soft, knowing smile.

I shook my head. "I wouldn't say I was very strong. Not for staying with Keith."

"You were surviving," she said without hesitation. "There's a difference."

Her words landed like a truth I wasn't ready to admit. I looked down at my hands, twisting the edge of my sleeve. Thinking I didn't feel strong. I felt bruised, ashamed, and small.

"Sometimes surviving is the strongest thing a person can do," Ms. Jones added, her tone steady. "And you're sitting here today, still breathing, telling your story. That's not weakness." I nodded slowly, the lump in my throat rising again.

"Maybe you didn't stay because you were weak," she said, "maybe you stayed because no one had ever taught you what strength in love is supposed to look like."

That line lingered in the air between us like incense smoke, light but heavy at the same time.

"I guess," I whispered. "I just wanted to be loved right. Was that really too much to ask?"

"No," she said softly. "It never was, nor is it too much now."

And in the silence that followed, for the first time in a long time... I didn't feel completely alone.

Part Five: I Didn't Miss Him. I Missed Myself

"I'd like to circle back to Keith," Ms. Jones said gently. "You mentioned going to court to determine the charges. How did that turn out? Did they agree to send him overseas?"

"Yes. The domestic violence charges were reduced to lesser charges, disturbing the peace." I gave a short laugh. "He disturbed my peace of mind, for sure."

Ms. Jones offered a gentle smile, the kind that sees through deflection but doesn't press. She recognized the humor for what it was, a shield. "Keith was sent overseas during your second pregnancy, correct? How were you feeling with him gone?"

"Things actually started to get better once he was gone. I was working full-time, found a new apartment, and had our son in daycare. His sergeant ordered him to send money to our joint account, which helped a lot. I also opened an account in my name to have something that felt like mine. Something secure. I was finally starting to feel in control of my life again. And that control felt... unfamiliar, but right.

I wasn't used to making decisions without fear trailing behind me. I didn't have to shrink myself or wait for his mood to pass like storm clouds. I could breathe again. They did let him know he could return for the delivery, which I had mixed feelings about."

"Why the mixed feelings?" Ms. Jones looks at me, asking.

"A small part of me was still craving the idea of what a family was supposed to look like, especially when bringing a baby into the

110

world, but things were good with gone. I was feeling mixed emotions."

"That is understandable, Nadia." Ms. Jones gives her usual soft smile. "The sergeant told him he could return when you went into labor?"

I nodded. "Yeah. That was the plan."

Ms. Jones glanced down at her notes, then looked up again. "Did he finally accept the baby was his?"

"I guess so."

"How was it when he came home for the birth?"

"When I went into labor, they called him so we could talk. While we were on the phone, he told me he wouldn't be able to come home; he'd gotten in trouble for fighting. He was upset that they broke their promise to let him return, even though he messed up, and I was upset that he didn't put me first and take accountability for his actions. So, he missed the birth of his daughter."

I paused, but not from pain but to speak the truth. "Honestly? There was a part of me that felt relieved. My mom and sister were with me, and the delivery went smoothly. Peaceful and full of love and smiles. I needed that, although I did wonder if something was wrong with me.

I wondered whether I should have missed him more. Like, shouldn't I have wished he were in the room when our daughter took her first breath? But I didn't. And that truth sat quietly with me, telling me it's okay. Okay to choose peace. Okay, to stop trying to save someone else, hoping they would love me. That I was OK."

Ms. Jones nodded gently. "Sounds like you were beginning to enjoy life while he was away… and maybe learning how to hold space to love yourself."

"Yes," I said, almost a whisper.

"I was finally in control for a change."

Part Six: The Cost of Hope

"Did you and Keith still talk to each other after the birth?" Ms. Jones asked softly.

"Yeah," I said with a small nod. "We talked on the phone almost every day. He apologized for his behavior, and I agreed, again, to try to work on the marriage. I wanted to believe things could change. I just felt like they needed to change, especially since we had children."

I exhaled slowly before continuing.

"Then, on his way back to the States, his unit had a weekend layover in another country. That same weekend, I went to the store to grab some groceries, only to have my bank card decline. When I called the bank, they told me my account was in the negative. I was confused at first, but then the teller explained they had to withdraw funds from my personal account to cover overdraft charges on the joint account. Keith had drained everything I'd saved in my account."

I looked down, remembering the ache of that moment. "I sat on the couch and finally just cried that day. It felt like no matter how much progress I made, I would always be trapped. I had tried so hard to build something of my own, to feel secure... and in a weekend, it was gone. I was so mad at the bank that they even linked my account to ours. That was my lesson to not open a safe account at the same bank as the joint."

Ms. Jones remained quiet, giving space for the pain to settle before gently asking, "How were things when he returned home? This was his first time meeting your daughter, right?"

113

"Yes. She was two months old when he finally got back. At first, things seemed okay. He was calmer, bonding with the baby and reconnecting with our son. But it didn't last. Old wounds, old habits... they resurfaced. We started arguing again, but... There were some good moments too."

I smiled faintly. "We would play video games together and take the kids to the park. I really tried, Ms. Jones. I didn't want to raise my children alone. So, despite the long list of negatives, I tried to hold on to the short list of positives."

"Hope?" she offered, her voice soft.

I nodded again. "Yeah. Hope. Maybe that's my flaw... I'm always hoping."

"Is hope the reason why you stayed?" Ms. Jones's question filled the room.

"No or maybe," I said slowly. "I stayed because I didn't want to be judged for divorcing. I didn't want to be labeled as another young couple who rushed into marriage and had kids." I paused for a quick moment to reflect. "Now that I'm saying it out loud... it sounds like I hoped I could be different than what society had already written for me. Like I could rewrite the stereotype if I just held on long enough."

Ms. Jones nodded, her voice calm and curious. "Are people's opinions of you important?"

I shifted in the oversized chair, her words echoing in my head. I kept turning them over, one by one. Eventually, I looked up and answered, "I guess it is important."

"Was that hard for you to admit?" Ms. Jones tilted her head slightly.

"Yes," I said, my voice quieter. "Because I always believed I didn't care what people thought about me. But it sounds like I might... I might care more than I thought. Maybe even too much."

"It's okay to care about what people think," Ms. Jones said gently. "Have you ever heard the saying, 'Sticks and stones may break my bones, but words will never hurt me?'"

"Yeah."

"Do you think that's true?"

I paused, then shook my head. "No. Words have hurt me."

She nodded with quiet understanding. "Me too. What people say, and how they say it, can shape how we see ourselves. But the real question becomes: are we living for them... or are we living for us?"

I looked down at the carpet, heart pounding a little at the truth settling in my chest. "I let Keith change so much of me," I said, barely above a whisper. "I wish I had walked away the first time I felt unhappy. I don't even understand why I stayed as long as I did."

"We can take a moment to explore this question," Ms. Jones said, her voice even and calm, "not to place blame, but to help you gain more clarity. Let me ask you this: Were you scared to be alone?"

I took a breath, letting the question sit. "I was okay being by myself," I said slowly. "But being alone with children... that scared me. Not because I didn't think I could do it, but because I knew how hard it would be, having grown up with a single mother and seen the struggle. Still, even with that fear, I shouldn't have stayed."

"That makes sense," Ms. Jones nodded. "Sometimes we don't fully understand the impact of a situation until we've stepped away from it. It's hard to see the weight we're carrying when we're still underneath it. But once we step out... the contrast is undeniable."

I felt tears building at the edges of my eyes, not quite falling, just... waiting. "I get so mad at myself," I admitted, voice shaking. "That it took so long to leave. That I accepted so much. I look back now and wonder who that version of me even was, how I could have stayed with someone who treated me that way."

Ms. Jones leaned forward slightly, her energy steady. "It sounds like you're grieving more than just the relationship. You're grieving the parts of yourself that got buried to survive it."

I looked up, startled a bit by how right that felt.

"That's okay," she continued. "Grief isn't just about the loss of a person; it's about the loss of who we were, or who we thought we were supposed to be. But the fact that you're sitting here, saying these words out loud, shows that part of you is coming back to life."

My chest tightened, but not in pain. In release. "I guess almost like a new birth or an awakening of some sort?"

Ms. Jones smiled. "Yes. An awakening. And awakenings rarely happen quietly. They usually come after something breaks open, sometimes slowly, sometimes all at once, but either way, they make room for who we're becoming."

I nodded, slowly. "I used to think healing was just about fixing the damage. But maybe it's more about meeting the version of me that was never allowed to exist before." I say, but in a sense questioning.

"That version has always been there," Ms. Jones said. "She's just been waiting for you to choose her."

This time, I didn't look away. I let that truth land, right in the center of my chest, because I could feel it. I was finally choosing myself.

Reflection

Resentment...

One tear I cry for the people who said you would hurt me.

Two tears for not listening.

One tear I cry for when you left me.

And two tears for staying...

Part Seven: Silence Has a Voice

"Sometimes we don't understand the situation we're in until we leave," Ms. Jones said gently. "It's hard to see what's right in front of us until it's no longer in front of us, and when we aren't trying to survive in it but just live."

"I'm mad at myself that it took so long to leave. When I look back now, I can't believe I stayed with him for so long."

"What motivated you to finally leave?"

I stared at the carpet for a moment before answering. "It wasn't one moment. It was a collection of them. But there was one night that changed everything..."

I took a slow breath.

"After putting the kids to bed, we started arguing again. I don't even remember what we argued about. I remember his voice kept rising, and my body was tense, as it always was when the storm came. This time, he backed me up against the patio door. We lived on the third floor with the first floor at the basement level." My voice trembled, but I kept going.

"As we were arguing, he told me to jump. He yelled out for me to kill myself. At first, I thought I had misheard him. But then he picked up his basketball, tossed it at me, and attempted to hit me. He picked the ball up and repeated, 'Go ahead. Kill yourself,' while striking me with the basketball. He started walking toward me, shouting louder. And I... I just jumped. No shoes. Just my pajamas.

But something told me if I didn't jump, he was going to push me." I paused.

"I landed hard on the grass and fell rolling on the ground, while scraping my arm on some random twigs and rocks. I got up and ran. I ran until I collapsed in the nearby park, then cried until I dozed off on a bench. I woke up maybe two hours later, and I went back to the apartment and knocked on the door."

Ms. Jones's voice was soft but steady. "And what happened?"

"He asked, 'Who is it?' When I said, 'It's me,' he laughed. He asked again as if it were a joke. He didn't even open the door right away. Just... left me standing there like I didn't matter."

She leaned in slightly. "What do you think he was doing while you were gone? Did he seem worried?"

I shook my head. "No,"

"He was sitting on the couch playing video games. And this was around one in the morning, so the kids were still sleeping. He laughed when he opened the door and said he figured I'd be back."

"That situation is what pushed you to leave?" Ms. Jones asked, her pen moving across her notepad.

"That was the start of me opening my eyes," I admitted. "But no, I didn't leave right away."

I paused, steadying my breath.

"The next situation happened a week later. Keith and I were in the kitchen arguing, again, this time about his past affairs. I was tired of pretending like everything was okay. I told him we couldn't keep ignoring what he did, and he yelled back at me, saying I needed to just get over it."

I swallowed hard, feeling the anger in my chest rise, remembering. "I had tossed my cup of juice into the sink and said I was getting in the shower. I walked to the bathroom, locked the door, and broke down crying. He banged on the door, demanding that I open it. I stayed quiet, hoping he would go away." I shifted in the chair.

"When I didn't respond, I heard him walk away. I thought I was safe. I turned on the shower and stepped in, trying to calm down. Then I heard something hit the floor."

"What was it?" Ms. Jones asked gently.

"The doorknob. He had taken it off. He kicked the door in, walked in, and grabbed me out of the shower. Threw me over his shoulder like I was nothing. I screamed, telling him to put me down."

"Where did he take you?" Ms. Jones asked softly.

"He took me to the bedroom and tossed me on the bed. I yelled for him to leave me alone, but he straddled over me and held my arms down. He kept yelling that I needed to get over it. Then he stopped. He just looked at me, straight in my eyes, and put his hands around my neck.

"I tried to move, but his 200-pound body pinned my 120-pound frame. I struggled to breathe. That burnt rubber taste returned to my mouth. My eyes didn't cry anymore; they burned. That's when I knew..." I paused.

"What was it?" Ms. Jones asked, gently interrupting.

"That I didn't have any more fight in me," I said. "I was tired. I lay there and allowed that moment to be my last. I was ready to accept my ending. My head fell to the left, and that's when I saw my babies. My son and daughter were standing in the doorway, crying. And something about their cries, it was like when you're in church, and the song hits you so deep, your soul rises. Their cries gave me the strength to fight back."

"Can you remember what your thoughts were in that moment?"

"I remember thinking, I'm not going to let this man raise my children. I kicked and pushed until his grip finally slipped from my neck. He grabbed my leg as I kept fighting, and then I heard it crack. The sound of my own body breaking. I screamed as he tore the ligaments in my knee. He jumped off me quickly, grabbed every phone in the house, and hid them on the top shelf of the closet. I collapsed to the floor, holding my knee, and my kids ran to me. They kept asking if I had an 'Ouchy.'" I blinked hard, remembering the pain I felt.

Ms. Jones sat still for a long moment, her pen no longer moving. Her expression wasn't just a professional concern; it was human. A kind of soft mourning for the pain I had survived. But also, something else: reverence. As if she were witnessing the sacred return of a woman who had once gone missing within herself.

"What you lived through," she finally said, "wasn't just trauma. It was terror. And yet... You found your voice in that moment. Even if it was just a whisper to yourself."

I nodded slowly, still sitting in the memory, still feeling my children's cries echoing in my ears.

She lowered her eyes, then gently asked, "How old were the children?"

"My son was almost three, and my daughter close to one," I answered, my voice a mix of heartbreak and clarity. "I explained to them that Mommy was okay. I held back tears until I could crawl into the bathroom. There was no door to shut, so I turned on the shower and balanced myself on one leg, trying to cry without sound. He basically did all this, and I didn't even finish showering and was fully naked."

Ms. Jones pressed her lips together before asking, "He didn't let you call for help, and he wasn't being mindful of the children seeing this?" She says, trying to keep her anger from showing.

"No," I said. "He didn't want me to call the police or my mom. When I turned off the shower, he came in, wrapped a towel around me, and said he wanted to help. I told him 'No,' but he picked me up anyway. He carried me back to the bedroom and sat me on the bed. Then he started pacing, saying it was my fault for fighting back. I dressed in a t-shirt and sweatpants and told him I needed to go to the hospital."

"And he agreed?" Ms. Jones asks.

"He said he would take me," I replied, pausing for breath. "But only if I promised not to tell the truth."

Part Eight: Facing the Silence

Ms. Jones leaned forward slightly. "How did you respond at the hospital when the nurse asked what happened?"

"I told them I fell... walking up the steps from doing laundry." The words came out quietly; my eyes fixed on the floor. "I wanted so badly to tell the truth. And I felt like they knew I was lying. The way they looked at me was gentle but cautious. Like they were waiting for me to admit it."

I swallowed hard. "I still wonder how life would've turned out if I had said, 'My husband hurt me.' Or when they ask you that routine question, 'Do you feel safe at home?' What would've happened if I had answered honestly and said, 'No... I don't feel safe?'"

I shook my head slowly. "Where would I be now, if I had spoken up for myself back then?"

Ms. Jones waited a moment before asking, "Do you regret not telling the hospital what really happened that day?"

"A piece of me does," I admitted. "A piece of me regrets not telling anyone what happened that day, or any day before that. But I was in survival mode as you've mentioned. My situation had me in a very lonely place. People love to say what they would or wouldn't allow. Hell, I even said it once. I used to say I'd never let a man put his hands on me."

I let out a bitter laugh. "But the truth is, until you're in it, until your whole world is twisted in fear and shame, you really don't know what you'd do. I always thought I'd be that strong, hard-ass woman who'd walk away the first time he crossed a line. But I didn't even realize I was being abused... until I left."

"Domestic violence happens more than it's ever reported," Ms. Jones said softly. "So many women are scared to admit what's happening, either out of fear or shame. And sadly, a lot of the judgment doesn't come from strangers. It comes from friends. Family. People who should offer support but instead offer blame." She paused. "And then there's the fear of what could happen if you speak up. That fear is real; that is why stories like yours matter. Your voice can help others recognize what's happening in their own lives, before it's too late."

"Yes," I nodded slowly, "I agree. But like you said... It's hard, especially when you're still in it. When you're scared about what could happen if you do speak up, and then not to mention who really would want to hear my story without passing negative judgment?" I say, shrugging my shoulders.

"In the hospital that day, I wanted to ask for help. I wanted someone to read between the lines of what I wasn't saying. But I didn't know who I could trust. I didn't even know who I could call. I felt so alone. And the scary part is... I knew that telling the truth could make things worse."

Ms. Jones leaned in, her presence grounding.

"I was discharged that same night. When I walked out into the lobby, there he was. Standing next to the stroller with the kids, as if nothing had happened. And just like that... I had no choice but to leave with him. Back to the same apartment. Back to the same silence. Back to protecting someone who wasn't protecting me." Ms. Jones was quiet for a moment before gently asking, "How were things when you returned home?"

"I was angry at Keith," I began, my voice tight. "But a part of me feared him even more. I felt like I had to stay. And the truth is, I don't even know why. It was like something had a hold on me.

124

Something I couldn't break free from, no matter how much I hated being there."

Ms. Jones leaned in slightly, her voice soft but steady. "This is good, Nadia. You're digging into the roots, and that's where the healing starts. Asking why you stayed, even when it hurts, is part of your healing journey. That should feel like progress."

"Yeah?" I gave a bitter laugh. "Because it doesn't feel good. Honestly, it makes me feel sick to my stomach. I look back at who I was and wonder... why? Why would I stay with someone like him, and again, I don't get it?"

My eyes welled with tears I refused to release. "I had no identity of my own. No voice to speak up. No legs to walk away. I stayed when I should've run. I was living in a prison without bars. On death row without a trial. And the worst part? I didn't even fight for my own life. I stayed with a man who attempted to take my life numerous times."

Ms. Jones let the silence linger, honoring the weight of what I'd said.

"That is a powerful truth," she said gently. "And it's yours. The moment you name what you felt is the moment you start reclaiming your power."

"More of that rebirth awakening stuff, huh?" I ask, trying to bring in a little humor to break the heaviness.

"Yes," Ms. Jones says, her eyes locking with mine. "More of that stuff."

There's a softness in her expression as she sees me. Not just me sitting in the chair, but the one I buried a long time ago. I look down at my shoes. My throat tightens, like it's trying to seal off any more truth from escaping. My palms are growing clammy. I can hear my own heartbeat louder than her voice as the words I just spoke echo inside me. Sentences I've never said out loud. Not to anyone. Not even to myself. Everything in me wants to run. To stand up, leave, and bury all this again. But I don't move. I feel stuck. Not because I'm trapped by someone else anymore…But because now, I must face myself.

"How are you feeling?" Ms. Jones asks, gently breaking the silence.

I exhale slowly. "I'm okay," I lie a little, before softening to the truth. "I think that was a lot to say out loud. It was only a few sentences, but it felt like… a lifetime of hurt and pain was finally coming out." I pause before speaking again. "This whole talking about my past, it's a lot."

"Sometimes saying just a few sentences can mean everything," Ms. Jones says gently. "How about we take a break here? I'd like you to take some time this week to focus on self-care."

I wrinkle my brow. "What is that exactly?"

"Self-care is taking time for you. Take yourself to dinner, go see a movie, read something that makes you feel good. Do something that brings you joy and lets your body and your spirit relax. You can even turn on some music and dance. You've made remarkable progress today. I'm proud of how far you've come. I hope you're proud too."

I nod slowly, feeling a small warmth bloom in my chest. "Thank you, Ms. Jones. I'll work on that this week. It has been a little while since I blasted some music and danced with myself. I guess a solo dance party is needed."

I stand and grab my purse. As I headed to the door, I paused and looked back at her.

"Thank you again. I'll see you next week."

Ms. Jones gave a friendly smile and nodded.

Outside, the air feels different. Not lighter, exactly. But it's clearer.

I walked to my car and stopped for a moment, just standing there. I take a deep breath, the kind that fills every corner of your lungs, and realize I haven't really breathed since I walked into that building.

Once in the driver's seat, I sat in silence for a few moments, staring ahead. I am considering texting Dasia. I even unlocked my phone. But something in me says, not yet. I put the phone down and started the car.

Then, quietly, I drove myself home.

Session Five

Part One: In Between

I pulled into therapy and put my car in park in front of the building, as my stomach started to knot up. I glanced at the clock. Twenty minutes early. I stared out the windshield, watching the breeze ruffle the leaves of the tree just outside the office. My fingers tightened around the steering wheel as my mind wandered. Was I talking too much about my past? Was I using therapy as a dumping ground, or was I really healing? Sometimes I wondered what Ms. Jones was thinking; was it compassion or disbelief? Did she silently question how one person could carry so much trauma?

My silent thoughts broke with a buzz from my purse.

I sighed, reached down, and pulled out my phone. Dasia's name appeared on the screen alongside her smiling photo. I stared at it, debating. Pick a fight or risk it, or ignore and pretend I still don't care? Also, telling myself I need to change her contact picture to a bug or something.

"Hello," I said flatly, already bracing myself.

"Sorry to call," she said quickly, her voice soft but shaky. "I just… I needed to hear your voice."

I closed my eyes, bracing for where this was about to go. "Okay." "Is this a bad time?" she asked, almost whispering.

"Kind of. I'm about to head into a meeting."

There was a pause, a sharp inhale. "I'm sorry. I just… do you think we could sit down and talk soon?"

"I'll let you know," I said, stepping out of the car, voice monotoned not to show much emotion.

"I'll take that," she said, and I could hear the hope through her words. "Are you going to a work meeting? How is work? I miss you so much. I miss hearing about your day."

I didn't answer right away. I hated how she always tried to slip back in as if nothing had happened. Even more, I hated that I missed her, too. "It's something like that," I finally muttered, pulling the door to the building open, the air inside cool and sterile against my flushed skin.

She didn't know I was walking into another therapy session. She didn't know I was about to break open the parts of myself she used to feed from, my fear of being alone. And maybe she didn't care. Or maybe… she did. But I couldn't get pulled into that again. Not today.

"Hello, I will let her know you are here," the receptionist says as I sign in.

"Are you seeing someone else?" Dasia nervously asks, "Because it sounded like another woman's voice."

"What? I am not getting into that with you right now. I will let you know about meeting up."

"Okay. Can I tell you something?"

"Sure?"

"I love you still despite all that's going on, and I understand if you no longer want to tell me anymore, but I wanted to tell you."

"Okay," I say. "I have to go now." I ended the call and placed the phone back in my purse.

Part of me wanted to scream at Dasia for even saying that. Another part wanted to hold on to those words, like a life raft, even if I didn't know if I wanted them. Maybe I just needed to feel wanted by someone, anyone, and feel like someone loved me.

The door opens, and Ms. Jones steps out with that same gentle expression she always wears. "Hello Nadia, come on back," she says softly.

I smile. "Hello," I say, walking to the door.

While walking down the hall, I pull my phone out to text Dasia. I type the words, "I love you too," then quickly hit delete and drop my phone back in my purse, clutching it like it's the only thing holding me together.

"How was your day?" Ms. Jones says as we walk into her office.

"It is fine," I reply, forcing a smile and sitting in the chair.

"Were you able to complete your homework?"

"Hmm, kind of, I think. I didn't take myself out anywhere, but I did take a bath and shaved my legs... if that counts."

Ms. Jones smiles warmly. "It counts if you spent time making yourself happy."

"Well, it counted for me because it's something that I feel I never have time for. It was nice to do the self-care thing."

"That is good to hear. I would like you to try and do something every week for yourself." Ms. Jones says, flipping pages in her notebook.

Part Two: The Weight of Leaving

"I would like to pick up where we left off." Ms. Jones says while writing in her notebook. "We were discussing how you were feeling when you came home from the hospital, but we were getting to what motivated you to leave."

"Okay. Well, after I came home from the hospital, things were tense in the house. I didn't say much and locked myself in the bedroom with my kids when we would fight. I also started to sleep with a knife under my pillow in case he attempted to kill me again.

It made it harder to sleep, knowing it was there, like I was one wrong move away from a different kind of nightmare, but it also gave me a strange sense of empowerment. I struggled with the thought of what it would mean if I had to use it, what that would look like for me."

Ms. Jones' eyebrows lifted slightly, but her voice stayed calm. "I can understand the mix of emotions. Did that help you feel safer? Did you call anyone during the fights, such as the police?"

"Yes and no about feeling safer. I would call the police, but they never took any action. They'd come to the house, tell me that since he was on the lease, they couldn't do anything, and it didn't help that he would mention his military service and returning from overseas. Keith would always be standing right there when the male officers arrived, and they would praise him for his service, unaware that he'd been given a dishonorable discharge. I would even tell them I was scared, but they always said I should find a safe place to go."

"I know that was hard, considering you tried to reach for help and felt unheard, again," Ms. Jones said, her tone steady but compassionate. "Did you open up to anyone else about what was going on besides the police?"

"No. I kept it a secret for months, until I was just... tired of living in fear. I finally spoke up and told my parents that I wanted to leave."

"Your dad was in the picture?"

"Yes, he was around again. He even said I could stay with him while I figured things out. I picked a day during the week because I wanted to make sure Keith was at work."

"Was he working in the military?"

"No. He was not active anymore. He was working at a factory about fifteen minutes from the apartment."

"Okay, so the dishonorable discharge meant he was kicked out?"

I nodded. "Yes."

"Did you take this chance to leave while he was at work?"

"Yes. I picked a Monday morning so he would have no choice but to keep working throughout the week. When he left, I quickly packed clothes for the kids and me. I put everything in my car and then waited in the apartment by the phone. He would always call during his lunch break. I watched the clock, my life depending on every second, but I guess it did in a way.

When the phone rang, I jumped, startled that this was it. I answered, trying to keep my voice steady. He was on the other end, asking what I was doing. I responded that I was cleaning the house and waiting for him to get off work, just like I always did.

After we hung up, I quickly grabbed the kids and strapped them into their car seats. As I drove, the fear set in, and I began to doubt what I had done. I started asking if I was doing the right thing. I pulled into a gas station and just sat there, hands gripping the steering wheel, wondering if I should turn around and go back home or keep moving forward."

"What made you want to go back?" Ms. Jones asked.

"I guess… I was scared of the unknown. Scared of him being mad."

"Maybe," Ms. Jones said softly, locking eyes with me, "you were scared of being free?"

Her words hit harder than I wanted to admit. Scared of being free. Maybe that was it. Maybe freedom wasn't just scary; maybe I didn't even know what it looked like to be free, not just then but even now.

Part Three: My Shadow Froze Me

Ms. Jones leaned forward slightly, her voice pulling me out of my thoughts. "What happened next? Once you chose to leave, how did you feel?"

"I felt empty," I said after a pause. "People talk about how leaving can make you feel happy, like a weight lifted off your shoulders, but I didn't feel that. Instead, it felt as if a heavier weight was placed on my shoulders. I was now on my own with two kids, no money, and no real home. I didn't have a plan because my only focus now was to stay alive."

"I thought you were working while he was overseas?"

"I was," I admitted, "but he always made it seem like everyone was flirting with me or I was messing around at work, so I felt I had to quit working once he returned home. It was just draining since I wasn't doing anything and never did anything to make him feel insecure. Like he was the one who did all the cheating, not me."

"Oh. Okay," Ms. Jones says, jotting something on her notepad. She looks back up at me. "What did you decide while at the gas station?"

"I left his ass!"

Her lips curve into a proud smile. "Good for you. You decided to move forward, unsure of what could or would happen next, but you did it. Life is about decision-making, and we all have the choice to go left or right. Sometimes we don't know if it's the right direction until later, but we make those choices in hopes that they lead to somewhere better, to a brighter path."

"You're right, Ms. Jones. When I decided to drive away, it opened more doors, and I had to keep choosing one after another. I stayed with my dad, and things were okay… until I started to miss him."

"Meaning, Keith?"

"Yes," I admitted, my voice quieter. "I was starting to second-guess myself again. I was missing a man I hated. I know that sounds so silly."

"What were you missing?"

I took a deep breath. "I think I was missing the comfort of my old life. I knew what to expect and how to go about my daily tasks. I knew what my day-to-day would look like. In a twisted way, it was my stability. And now… I was a single mother working random part-time jobs, and needing the help of the government to feed my children."

"Did you go back?"

"No, I didn't go back… but that didn't matter."

Her pen stopped moving. "What do you mean it didn't matter?"

"It didn't matter because he kept finding me. I moved out of my dad's place and found a place of my own with my mom's help. Somehow, he found out where I lived, I guess by following me because I never told him the address.

One night, he sat outside my house when I returned home from a little friend-type date. The guy who took me out helped carry my kids inside since they'd fallen asleep in the car. I was unlocking

the door when Keith came running out of the shadows. Before I could react, he snatched our son from the guy's arms and barked at me to take the kids inside. My body froze. For a split second, I wasn't that free woman; I jumped to his commands and felt terrified.

Then instinct kicked in. I scrambled, almost dropping my keys, quickly taking my babies inside my apartment to the couch.

When I ran back out, Keith was on top of him. His fists moved like they had a mind of their own. I screamed, but my voice sounded far away, like I was underwater. He didn't stop. The streetlights allowed me to see blood pouring from the guy's face. My hands were shaking as I called the police, praying they'd hurry, but Keith took off before they ever showed up."

"Oh wow. Did you remain in contact with this guy?" Ms. Jones asked.

"No. He wanted nothing to do with me after that. I was angry... but I understood. This guy was one of the good ones, but like everything good in my life, my past finds me and takes it away."

Part Four: My Therapist is a Detective

"How did you meet him?"

"He worked at a video store where I'd go rent movies, back when renting movies at a store was still a thing."

Ms. Jones smiles. "Yes, I remember those days. What made him a good guy?"

"His heart," I said without hesitation. "When we started talking, I was no longer living at my dad's. It wasn't working out, probably because I only knew how to run. My kids and I were basically living out of my car for a little over a month before my mom helped me get a place of my own."

"The apartment is where Keith beat up your date?"

"Yes." My throat tightened. "My mom helped me get that apartment. Before that, I stayed in a motel for as long as I could afford, just a few days. When he and I first started talking, I had just left my dad's. I spent a few nights at the motel, then went to the shelter."

Ms. Jones tilted her head slightly. "How was that?"

"Overwhelming," I admitted. "They were full, so the only space left was a single bottom bunk bed for the three of us. I lay in bed holding both my kids until they fell asleep. While in the dark, I could hear the other women crying softly." "Why do you think they were crying?"

"It sounded like hurt, pain, confusion... At least those were the reasons I wanted to cry." My voice faltered. "It's terrifying to leave

137

your home and end up in a place full of strangers. We were all there because of domestic violence, but we weren't there together. It felt like everyone was trapped in their private hell."

Ms. Jones nodded gently. "Hearing them must have been hard on you."

"It was. So I went to the bathroom and called my guy friend. He just listened while I cried and vented, which I wasn't used to. He prayed with me and told me everything would be okay. After the call, I went back to the room and held my kids until I saw sunlight creeping through the blinds."

"How was the next day?"

"After breakfast, I met with the social worker to talk about my next steps. But I still felt so overwhelmed. So that evening, I called him again. To talk and not unload again on him."

"You called your guy friend?"

"Yes. But when he answered, he said my situation was weighing heavily on him, just hearing me cry like that. Then he offered to pay for a couple more nights at a motel so I wouldn't have to go back to the shelter. It gave me a small break, but after those nights, my kids and I were back on our own."

"Where else were you sleeping during that time?" Ms. Jones asked gently.

"Anywhere we could," I admitted. "Mostly motels when I could afford them. Sometimes I'd drive around at night and let my kids sleep in the back seat of my car because I was scared the cops would toss me in jail if they found out we were homeless. Granted, I now realize the police wouldn't have, but I didn't trust them to look out for me. I stayed with family here and there, but it was never stable. Sometimes, I'd sleep in my car between classes. We just… survived until my mom could help me get a place. Which ended up being the place Keith found me."

Ms. Jones let out a soft sigh. "You were in college during this time?"

"Yes. I started community college because I felt like the only way I could ever provide for my kids was to get a degree. I had to do something to give me hope." I shrugged, staring down at my hands.

Her voice softened, almost breaking. "That had to be so much to carry, being homeless, caring for two children, trying to build a future... and still needing to feel safe."

"Looking back now, I guess I didn't take time to think; I just did it. I felt like if I sat around thinking, I would've felt sorry for myself instead of focusing on getting out of that situation." I exhaled deeply without meaning to.

Ms. Jones tilted her head. "Why the deep breath?"

I blinked at her, caught off guard. "I... I don't know. It just happened."

"People tend to take a deep breath when they're feeling something they can't quite show," she said softly. My chest tightened. "What do you mean?"

"Do you have a hard time expressing how you feel?"

I broke eye contact, staring at the floor. "Hmmm... sometimes I think I do express how I feel. But people take advantage of you once you open up. Other times, people don't understand what I'm trying to say. So, I learned not to show my emotions. I don't want anyone to use my feelings against me. So... I keep it to myself."

I paused, almost whispering. "To answer your question... I don't think I have any trouble expressing it. I don't trust that I can express my emotions to anyone and that they care."

139

"I've noticed something," Ms. Jones said gently. "As we have been speaking, you haven't shed a single tear during our sessions, even when talking about some very intense situations. Would you say this is how you normally handle emotions?"

I shifted uncomfortably. "Crying is a sign of weakness to me. I always felt like if I sat around crying, people would just feel sorry for me, and I don't want that. I don't want anyone to look at me differently or use my pain against me. So I hold it in. If I keep my head down and push through, no one pays too much attention. I'm not saying I never cry... I just don't do it often or around people."

Ms. Jones tilted her head. "What makes you think they would only feel sorry for you?"

I let out a bitter laugh. "Because society always feels sorry for the girl who's struggling. The poor girl. I didn't want to be judged like that. And I didn't want anyone pointing fingers and telling me what I should've done differently. So... when I did cry, I did it alone. I mean, you see what happened when I couldn't control myself with my guy friend, he basically felt sorry for me."

Ms. Jones' voice softened even more. "When you did cry... did you want someone there? Or even now, would you like someone to just sit with you and listen?"

I wanted to take another deep breath, but now I knew Ms. Jones was watching my every move. I tried not to make any sudden movements. This lady was making my underarms sweat. I couldn't even fan out my shirt because she'd probably call that out, too. If I glanced at my phone, would she analyze that as well? Ms. Jones wasn't a therapist; she was a damn detective. Or a scientist dissecting my every move like a lab rat.

"You look deep in thought. Are you okay?" Ms. Jones asked.

"Yes," I said quickly. "I was just sitting here thinking about your question."

140

"Were you able to come up with an answer?"

I hesitated, then nodded slightly. "Just… that everyone wants someone there for them. So I guess I would like that sometimes. I mean, I don't think my needs are much different from everyone else's." I shifted in my seat, almost embarrassed.

Part Five: I'm Coming Out...

"I would like to shift some. On your first day in the office, you mentioned having a partner. Is this partner a man or a woman, if it's okay for me to ask?"

"She's a woman."

Ms. Jones nodded. "Is she the first woman you've been with?"

"No, she isn't my first."

"Sounds like you were able to explore your sexuality?" Ms. Jones says with a warm smile. "The curiosity never left?"

"Yes... and no, it didn't. The last few months I was with Keith, I started having a lot of dreams about being with women. I struggled with my sexuality and thought something was wrong with me."

Ms. Jones leaned forward slightly, her tone soft. "Nothing is wrong with you at all. Why don't you tell me about your first experience? I want us to cherish this part of your life because it is important."

I nodded slowly. "Okay... well, one of my close guy friends told me he had a friend with children and thought we'd get along."

"He had a female friend?"

"Yes. He knew I wanted to make new friends. He brought her over one day, and we all talked while the kids played together.

Her name was Tina, and we clicked instantly. We started talking on the phone and hanging out a lot. We didn't share the same lifestyle, but we both wanted a better life, and we bonded through our trauma. Then one night while we were on the phone, she said she needed to ask me a question."

Ms. Jones gave a small, encouraging smile. "And how did you feel in that moment?"

I let out a giggle, remembering how I had felt in that moment. "Honestly? I didn't think anything of it. We'd been opening up to each other so much already... I just thought it was going to be something simple like another life story to share or something about the kids."

"Was that what she wanted to talk about?"

"Nope. She asked if I'd ever been with a woman, and I freaked out. I mean, stomach in knots and everything," I say, giggling at the memory again. "I blurted out, 'No way!' and went on about how that's not right and I would never do something like that. Then I quickly gave a reason to hang up. But as soon as I hung up, I just lay there, shocked... and upset with myself for lying. I lied to her and myself.

So, I texted her and asked her to call me back. When she did, I asked her to repeat the question. She sounded confused until I explained that I wanted her to ask me again what she'd asked before we hung up.

She asked again if I'd ever thought about messing with a woman, and this time, I told her the truth. I said, 'Yes.'"

"How did it feel to be honest? That had to be a lot to admit out loud."

"I don't know. I guess it just felt... strange, saying it out loud to someone," I admitted, fidgeting with my hands. "I spent most of my life trying to bury it, hoping it would disappear, but it never did. So, yes, I'd say it was a lot to admit out loud to someone else and myself."

"Hoping what would go away?" Ms. Jones asked gently, tilting her head as if to encourage me to go deeper.

"Being attracted to women," I said after a pause, my voice dropping. "Wanting to be more than just a friend. Struggling with myself, wondering why I couldn't just be 'normal.'"

"You feel having an attraction to someone of the same sex isn't normal?" she asked, her tone calm and curious.

"Yes, because society made me feel that way," I confessed. "But I don't anymore. This is who I am. God doesn't make mistakes. People do. They twist God's love into judgment, picking and choosing what they think is right and wrong." I paused, staring at the floor. "And it hurts… it really hurts when someone who claimed to care suddenly turns their back on you just because of your sexuality. I'll never fully understand that, but I've learned that people often love conditionally, while God loves unconditionally."

Ms. Jones nodded, letting the silence stretch for a moment before she asked, "Was it hard for you to 'come out?'"

I laughed lightly, but it sounded more like a sigh. "Hard? It felt impossible at first. I carried so much shame. I thought if I could just keep it hidden, I could stay safe… but hiding only made me feel more alone. It wasn't one big 'coming out' moment for me. It's been a series of little steps, learning to tell the truth about who I am, even when it feels terrifying. And yet it felt as if I were living different lives with different people. At church and with some family, I played the role they saw as 'normal,' but with others, I could finally breathe and just be myself. It was draining… and honestly, depressing."

I looked up at her and added, "You know, Ms. Jones, I never really understood the term 'coming out.' We don't ask heterosexuals, 'When did you come out?' Society is so obsessed with fitting people into these black-and-white boxes that no one pauses to see the shades in between, the ways people actually live and love. I didn't 'come out' in the way people think of it. I just… told the truth. That

144

day, on the phone with Tina, I was finally being honest about who I am. I am a bi-racial lesbian woman, figuring out life just like everyone else.

Ms. Jones tilted her head slightly with a soft smile. "Does your sexuality define who you are?"

I answered without hesitation. "My sexuality says that I am attracted to women, but it doesn't define who I am as a person. I'm not afraid to stand out in society just because someone else doesn't understand. Shit, I can't even understand how someone can sleep with a man, and honestly, it grossed me out while I was doing it. One of my best friends is a guy, so this isn't me bashing men. It's just… I can't be with one in an intimate way. It's not who I am, not to mention the scent of a woman is amazing, so yes, in a way, my sexuality defines who I am attracted to, but doesn't explain who I am as a human."

"You made many great points, and I appreciate your sharing. I agree that whoever someone loves doesn't define a person's soul. I would like to know, once you were honest with Tina, how she responded?"

"She laughed at me and said she already knew. I guess I gave off that vibe of gayness," I said, laughing at myself. "We ended up talking on the phone a little longer. She told me she was interested in me and wanted to explore being more than friends. I remember feeling so nervous. She was leaving for a month to help her family, and I told her that once she got back, I'd be ready. She agreed and said she was looking forward to coming back."

Ms. Jones leaned in slightly. "Ready for what?" she asked with curiosity.

"Ready to… talk to a woman and try stuff, I guess," I said, laughing again, while my hands fidgeted in my lap. "Basically, explore what being more than just friends actually looks like."

"Were you interested in this woman as well?" Ms. Jones asked, her voice even and inviting.

"Yeah," I admitted, a smile tugging at my lips. "She was pretty, and I had a lot of fun hanging out with her. We would laugh for hours, just losing track of time. We liked the same kinds of movies, and music… also we both had kids around the same age, so we understood each other in ways that made it easy to connect."

"It sounds like you two had a few things in common. While she was gone for that month, did you two continue to talk?" Ms. Jones asked.

I burst out laughing. "Not exactly. She called me the very next day and said she didn't have to go out of town after all, and that she was on her way to my house. I remember freezing, thinking I had time to prepare, but I had only twenty minutes. I said okay, hung up the phone, and tried to stay calm."

"Oh wow, what a change of plans," Ms. Jones said, smiling.

"Yes, I would agree. A change I was not mentally ready for," I said, giggling. "I needed mental preparation… and a shower." Ms. Jones chuckled softly. "So, what happened when she came over?"

I took a deep breath and laughed again. "Well… I had my first experience with a woman. And honestly? It was awful. I had no idea what I was doing or what to expect. But hey, I made it through alive, so that's all that matters, right?"

"That is one way to look at it," Ms. Jones said with a soft smile. "Did this turn into your first same-sex relationship?"

"We didn't officially call it a relationship until later," I admitted. "But we continued to hang out a lot. And for the first time, I felt like I could open up… even about Keith."

I paused, realizing how heavy that name still felt on my tongue. But at that moment, I also felt something lighter, like telling my story out loud was the first step toward really owning it.

Part Six: Freedom With a Splash of Anger

"Did you ever hear from Keith again?"

"I did. We were finally going through a divorce, so we saw each other sometimes," I said, shrugging. "But we weren't always allowed in the courtroom at the same time because of the protection order."

"Protection order?" Ms. Jones asks, looking at me.

"Yes. I finally went forward with getting a protection order to stay away."

"Good for you. How did you feel about moving forward with the divorce?"

"I felt okay."

Ms. Jones tilted her head. "I want you to take time and really think about that before you respond," she said gently. "How did you feel about divorcing Keith?"

I repeated the question in my head a few times before answering. "I was happy… happy to start living a life where I didn't have to fight every day or be scared that he would hurt me. But I felt relieved not to walk on eggshells in the same house. I was scared, too, scared because I was about to start a new life. But I was…umm… happy about the divorce."

Ms. Jones let the silence stretch. "What else did you feel about the divorce?"

"I guess I was a little angry, but I was fine," I said, my gaze dropping to the floor.

"Angry about what?"

"I don't know… angry he put me through so much."

"Can you explain more about this anger you felt?"

"I don't know, just angry."

"Maybe take a moment to think about how you felt," Ms. Jones quickly replied, her tone calm but insistent.

I could feel myself starting to get mad, and my chest tightened. She wasn't going to let this go. I wasn't used to this, sitting in my feelings instead of shoving them back down where I kept them. It made me uncomfortable, as if she were trying to expose me. I looked up at her, my voice sharper. "I was angry at him for messing up the family he claimed he wanted. He wanted a damn family so bad, but couldn't step up to the plate. Like, why beat me down for having an abortion, but he couldn't even be a real father or husband? I was so mad at him for making me feel like shit all those years. I didn't know who I was anymore. I couldn't even look at myself in the mirror because I didn't recognize the woman staring back."

I paused before continuing. "I allowed this man to break me in so many ways that I became embarrassed by who I was. I had to even ask my mother if I was still pretty. I was in such a dark place and had no idea how I let that happen. But when our divorce was final, I started to live life for the first time, and those fears I had gone away because reality was I had always been a single mother in a relationship. I just needed to accept that and step away."

I exhaled hard. "So yeah… I was happy."

Ms. Jones nodded, jotting something down on her notepad. "What did you do?" she asked softly.

"What do you mean? Do when?"

"After the divorce," Ms. Jones clarified, leaning forward slightly. "What path did you take with your new freedom?"

Reflection

In a Moment

You held out your hand, and I grabbed it.

For a moment, I felt true happiness.

I understood love and how it's supposed to feel.

For a moment, I could touch the skies.

For a moment, I felt so alive!

Your love gave me wings to soar so high.

You climbed over my walls and found your way into my heart.

For a moment, I smiled at the feeling you gave me…

…and in a second, it was gone.

In a second, you left me confused and hurt.

In a second, I built my wall a little higher…

…so the next moment won't happen again.

Part Seven: Sitting With the Truth

"I started to party," I admitted. "Meeting new people... random people. Even reconnected with people from my past. At the time, I thought I was really living life. But looking back now, I know I was numbing myself. Still... it was fun while it lasted, I guess."

Ms. Jones nodded, jotting something down. "What were some things you were doing to 'live life?'"

"Well... I found myself drinking almost every day and partying, either at clubs or at my house. I experienced life in a way I'm not exactly proud to talk about today. It's... embarrassing. But I did it, so I'm just taking the good out of the bad."

"Do you feel safe talking about it now?" Ms. Jones asked gently.

"Umm... I feel safe saying it, but I can't actually admit what I did. That feels embarrassing."

Ms. Jones leaned forward slightly. "Can you help me understand the difference? What feels different between talking about it and admitting it?"

I took a deep breath. "Talking about it feels... safe. Because I don't judge anyone else who's lived that kind of life, made those choices, or is living it now. So, saying it out loud, it's just sharing an experience. Like talking about a situation you know about. But admitting it?" I paused, staring at my hands.

"Admitting it means I can't distance myself from it, basically saying that the situation is mine. And that's embarrassing because people

151

put me on this pedestal, like I was the 'good one' who did no wrong. Like it's not expected of me to do anything to that degree. Whatever that means."

Ms. Jones nodded thoughtfully. "Thank you for explaining that, and I understand it. I would like to know what that version of living felt like for you, or what you learned about yourself?"

"I learned to enjoy drinking a lot," I admitted. "Which eventually led to other things, other drugs. Mainly smoking."

"Smoking what?" Ms. Jones asked, her tone even.

"Marijuana," I responded, my gaze dropping to the ground as shame crept over me. "I also had no real income at the time, so… I started dancing. I was hanging around a fast crowd, but my life felt like it was moving in slow motion during that time." "Dancing meaning… a stripper?" Ms. Jones asked gently.

"Not a stripper at a random club," I said quickly. "But doing private shows here and there and..." I paused, then sighed. "Never mind. Yes… a stripper. See? Personally, that's so embarrassing to say out loud." I let out a nervous laugh. "But I kind of had fun. The sad part is, I had to numb myself with alcohol and stuff to get through it, to be able to dance in front of random people. I'm an introvert, so doing that felt like becoming a completely different person, which I had to do. But I battled with the idea of being judged the whole time."

"What made you continue dancing if you felt uncomfortable?"

"It started as something fun to do one night, just a way to make a few dollars for groceries and rent," I explained. "But once I saw how easy it was to get money, it became a little hard to walk away. I told myself I needed the funds to survive."

"How long did you dance? Or are you still dancing?"

I laughed. "No, I'm not dancing. Nobody wants to see me out there dancing now." I giggled. "My kids are teenagers now, they would flip. They would yell now if they knew what I used to do to buy diapers and food." I laugh again.

Ms. Jones smiled. "That's funny. So when did you stop dancing?"

"I stopped years ago," I said, shrugging lightly.

"What encouraged you to stop?"

"My next relationship," I said. "Raya, she made me pick between her and dancing. She told me if I needed money, I needed to get a real job, verbatim."

"Sounds like she was blunt," Ms. Jones observed with a soft smile.

"She is outspoken and straight to the point. She gave me no choice because I really liked her. So I stopped dancing and started looking for a job."

"How did you two meet?"

"I met Raya on a social media site back when they were starting to become a thing. Remember MySpace, where you could pick wallpaper and a song? I don't remember exactly how we came across each other's page, but somehow, we started talking as friends, then flirting. I then asked if she wanted to meet in person at a café, and she agreed. We met in person, and the vibe was everything. We clicked so fast, and I told her I was going to end my relationship to pursue her."

"Did you end your relationship?" Ms. Jones asks, leaning in closer.

"I did." I pause, thinking of Raya again, and smile.

"I haven't seen that type of smile before. Speaking on Raya must be bringing up something special."

I catch myself smiling and begin to pull it back. "Yeah, that's a relationship I haven't spoken too much about or even tried to think about."

"Why is that?"

"I don't know. I guess it was so great that it hurt a lot, too. Guess another moment where I decided to tuck it away. Honestly, I was shocked she even gave me the time of day, given the situation I was in when we met. I looked up to her... she seemed like she was on the right track in life, and my life was a total wreck."

"What was going on?" Ms. Jones asked, taking a sip of her tea.

I smiled knowingly. "That might need to wait until next session. It'll open up a whole new subject. And I've learned you like to dig deep into my stories. But I will say I think Raya is a soul mate... whatever that means."

"It is only to understand you better," Ms. Jones said with a soft smile. "Okay, we can wait until next session. I take it you and this woman are no longer together?"

I let my thoughts drift back again before responding. "No, we aren't together, but it was a relationship that I hold close to me."

Ms. Jones peeks at her watch, "Is there anything else you'd like to discuss before we wrap up?"

"Not that I can think of. I just feel like I'm doing so much talking, too much, and I'm not used to discussing my life like this. I'm a very private person."

"You are not talking too much," Ms. Jones reassured me. "You're doing a great job of opening up. You're making real progress in therapy; you should be proud of yourself."

I smirked a little. "So I'm thinking we can start wrapping this therapy stuff up, and you just tell me what I should do in my current situation."

Ms. Jones chuckled lightly. "Therapy doesn't quite work like that. But with continued progress, I am confident you'll know what to do in your situation. We'll begin discussing it soon. I just wanted to take a moment to learn what makes you... you. A person's past shapes who they are today.

When we rush past that, we miss the root of why you react, feel, and choose the way you do now. Understanding your past gives you the tools to heal the parts of you that were hurt, and it helps you step into decisions with clarity rather than fear. That's why this work matters."

"I guess that is understandable. So I will see you later?" I ask, standing up.

"Yes, have a good rest of the day and remember to do some self-care."

"You too, and I will try," I respond, leaving the small office.

Session Six

Part One: When NO Meant Nothing

"Hello, Ms. Jones. How was your weekend?" I asked as I walked into the office and settled into the chair.

"It was a blessing. I was able to spend time with my family. Thank you for asking," she replied warmly. "How was your weekend?"

"That's always nice. I had a good weekend. It never seems to last long enough," I said with a quick smile.

"That is very true." Ms. Jones opened her notebook. "Are you ready to pick up from our last session? We were discussing your life in terms of starting to party and dance after the divorce. You mentioned engaging in things like drugs and alcohol, and the ultimatum your ex-girlfriend, Raya, gave you to stop dancing. We can also use this time to talk more about your relationship with Raya."

I took a deep breath. "I really don't want to open that door right now if that's okay." I glanced at the floor. "But after my divorce, before I met my girlfriend, I lived a lifestyle that felt good in the moment. But when those moments started to turn into reality, I'd numb myself, so I didn't feel anything. That was basically my life during that time."

"What do you mean by numbing?" Ms. Jones asked gently. "Numbing can mean different things to different people. If you don't mind, I'd like to know what it meant for you."

I looked down at my hands. "I guess... sex, alcohol, and drugs," I said quietly. "I was having a lot of sex with women. Most of them I barely knew, and honestly, I liked it that way. I didn't want a connection. It was easier to protect myself. I didn't want to feel anything emotional. Just instant satisfaction."

I paused, swallowing hard. "I was lonely... and sex made me feel close to someone in those moments, but never close enough to actually give them my heart."

"But for some reason, I have a feeling Raya was different, but we don't have to open that yet. Why do you feel you kept your heart closed off?"

"Raya was different. I felt emotions with her that scared me and made me feel safe at the same time. Raya and I were best friends at the core, which made a difference. But honestly, I kept my heart at a distance because I was tired of being hurt by people," I said, my voice holding back emotions. "I used to write about love in poems... but I never felt like I truly experienced it, but oddly I felt like I knew about it. Every time I got close enough to really feel it, the person would hurt me. Then they'd expect me to forgive them... so that they could do it again."

"Do what?"

"Hurt me."

The knot rose in my throat, fast and hard. I could feel tears forming, pushing against the walls I was trying to keep up. I sat there in silence, trying to keep myself together, trying not to let the weight of this topic break me open. Thinking about Raya...thinking about feeling lonely and thinking about my life over the years.

"Are you okay?" Ms. Jones asked, her eyes filled with concern.

"Yes, I'm okay," I said after a moment. "Just... thinking about everything and even how I was still talking to both men and women during that time, hoping love would find me, no matter the gender. I went on dates with both guys and girls, but it always felt hard to find someone who was truly into me. I know it sounds silly, but I felt as if a part of me were searching for someone. I don't know, I just wanted to be loved, I guess."

"You don't sound silly at all. You were looking for love. That's not silly, that's human. You were searching for love. Were you physically attracted to both men and women?"

"No, not really, just women. Well…" I hesitated, glancing away. "When I was dancing one night, I met a local rapper who was at the club. We talked a bit and laughed at silly things; it was nice. He made me feel beautiful in that moment."

"This was before the girlfriend asked you to stop dancing?"

"Yes, this was before I met her."

"Okay," Ms. Jones nodded. "So, you met this guy during your performance?"

"Ms. Jones, it wasn't a performance like that," I respond, laughing. "I was just hired to dance, but I appreciate you making it sound more professional," I smile. "Anyways, he was sweet, and we exchanged numbers so we could get to know each other better. After talking on the phone a few times, he asked me on a date, dinner, and a movie."

"That sounds nice," Ms. Jones said.

"Yeah, I thought so too. I remember feeling so excited because this guy was extremely well-mannered and not bad-looking, and crazy enough, I've not really been asked out on real dates. It's always just been hanging out, then we're together type of thing. But I agreed. When the night of our date arrived, he picked me up on time, but we drove back to his house because he still needed to finish getting ready. I sat in the living room while he showered. I was so sure I had found a good one; his place was clean and organized, everything in its place. I was sitting there on the black leather couch, looking around, when he came out with a towel wrapped around his waist. He glanced at the time and said we needed to make a run real quick.

"I asked where, and he told me he needed to check on his club. Turns out, he was a local rapper and also one of the owners of a strip club in the city. I asked if we were still going to make it to dinner. He said we might only make it to the movie, but we could grab some food. Then he disappeared into his bedroom to finish getting dressed. I remember feeling a little disappointed… but I tried to keep a positive attitude because I understand things pop up sometimes."

"He changed the plans without asking if it was okay with you?"

"Nope," I said. "We drove straight to the club. And no, it was not a club I danced at," I added with a half-smile, just in case she was wondering.

"I wasn't going to ask," Ms. Jones said with a grin.

"Well, when we arrived, I sat at the bar while he went in the back to handle whatever he needed to do. The bartender and I made small talk as I waited… and waited. After about 45 minutes to an hour, he finally came back out and said, 'Okay, let's go.'

We left the club and drove back to his house because, apparently, he'd forgotten something. I sat back down on the couch while he disappeared into his bedroom. After a while, I called out to ask what time we were going to the movie. That's when he said we'd have to see it another day; we'd missed it.

I remember sitting there, feeling the disappointment sink in. The date I'd been looking forward to all week had completely fallen apart. I got myself so excited about the idea of a real date and, once again, felt disappointed, but was more upset with myself for getting so excited in the first place. But I said, 'It's okay.'"

Ms. Jones tilted her head. "I'm sorry you were let down. What did he need to go home and get?"

"I don't know… nothing, I guess," I said with a slight shrug. "Because he came out of his room, sat next to me, grabbed my face, and started kissing me."

"Did you engage in the kiss?"

"I kissed him back a little, but then I tried to pull away because I didn't feel comfortable. I asked him if he could drive me home. He said, 'Yeah, in a little while,' then took off his shirt and pressed his body against mine. I tried to keep myself sitting up, but his weight pushed me back into the couch. I remember hoping he wasn't trying to have sex with me, so I asked him to get up."

"Did he get off you when you asked?"

"No, instead, he continued to kiss my neck while rubbing his hands on my body. I tried to wiggle away as he held me down, saying he knew I wanted it. I told him that I didn't want it and was ready to go home. He took his pants off and unbuttoned mine. I tried to put my hand in his way, so he was unable to pull down the zipper, but he pushed my hands out of the way. He started to get upset and yelled at me that he had to finish because he couldn't be left like that."

"Meaning that he was sexually aroused, so it was up to you to help him?" Ms. Jones asks, shaking her head.

"Exactly. He then pulled off my pants and pressed his body on mine again. He started having sex with me, I told him 'stop' a few times, but after being ignored. I just asked if he would please use protection, and he told me no because I felt too good to stop."

"What did you do?"

"I just lay there, praying that he would hurry because I wanted to go home. He continued, then told me he wasn't going to stop until I had an orgasm. I told him I wasn't going to and that I wanted to go

home, but he didn't respond again. I realized I had to fake an orgasm so that it would be over. I faked it, pretending
I was satisfied. He rolled himself onto the floor, breathing deeply.
I stood up, walked to the bathroom, and locked the door."

"Did he say anything to you?"

"No. I just went to the bathroom and sat on the toilet, hoping all his semen would drop into the toilet. I wanted no parts of him left inside me. Then I attempted to wash myself with wet toilet paper. Once I finished, I walked out of the bathroom and back to the couch. He finally got up and said someone was on the way to take me home, then stepped into the shower to freshen up before stepping back out. I sat on the couch silently. About a half hour later, he opens his bedroom door to say my ride is there to take me home."

"Did he walk you out to this person's car?"

"Nope. I just walked myself to the car and got in."

Part Two: The Cost of Survival

"That could have been very dangerous. Did he at least give you an idea of who was picking you up?"

"I know," I said, shaking my head. "But I just wanted to get home. And no, I wasn't sure, I just got in the car. Luckily, it was an older woman. Honestly, it was his mother. She did little errands or whatever for him. That's what I learned on the ride home."

"Oh wow," Ms. Jones said. "What happened when you left? Did you file a report?"

"I went home, showered, then went to sleep. A few days later, I went to my doctor's office and told them I needed to be checked for any diseases… but I didn't tell anyone what exactly happened. I never filed a report. I was too embarrassed."

"Why did you feel embarrassed?"

"Because I was so excited about going on a date… only to end up getting raped."

Ms. Jones leaned forward slightly, her voice calm but full of compassion. "Nadia, I want to pause here. First, I'm so sorry that happened to you. What you experienced was a violation, and it was not your fault. I know it can feel like embarrassment or shame belongs to you, but it doesn't. That embarrassment and shame belong to the person who chose to harm you, not to you for being excited or trusting someone. Your feelings right now are valid, but I want you to hear me clearly: you did nothing to deserve what happened."

I nodded slowly, feeling my throat get dry and my stomach tighten.

Ms. Jones continued, "Sometimes, after an experience like this, people avoid talking about it or reporting it because they're trying to protect themselves from more pain, judgment, or fear. That's a normal trauma response, but I also want you to know that speaking about it here is a step toward taking some of that power back."

She let a moment of silence pass before gently asking, "At any point after that night... did you hear from him again?"

"He would call and say how he'd like us to hang out again. I wanted so badly to yell at him about what happened... but I guess a piece of me was scared. I tried really hard to speak up for myself and told him I didn't consent to having sex that night, but he laughed it off, saying that I got off too. I felt so shitty. After that, when he called or texted, I ignored it until he finally stopped. I was tired of getting hurt by people."

"Did you feel like you were always getting hurt by people?"

"Yes," I said without hesitation. "I was tired of being lied to and cheated on and just made to look stupid. I feel like when I get hurt, I end up looking dumb."

"You felt dumb when people would hurt you?"

"Yes."

"Why is that?"

I took a breath. "Because I would like people and want to be serious... but they never seemed to feel the same way. For example, my first female relationship, Tina, the one that helped me admit my sexuality, well, she had so much going on, like bad situation after another, but despite everything, I stayed. I thought that if someone could love you in your weakness, then they'd also love you when you were strong. But I learned the hard way, sometimes when I loved someone while they were weak, it was just a distraction for them

163

until they no longer needed me." I shook my head. "She betrayed me, and it hurt... like it always does."

Ms. Jones tilted her head slightly. "How did she betray you?"

I sighed, remembering that day. "My guy friend that introduced us started dating a friend of hers, who was lying to him about her age. They told me not to say anything, but she was underage. I told him anyway, and he ended the relationship. A few days later, Tina called me to come over. I drove there with my four-year-old son in the front seat. This was, of course, when car seat laws were different, and people didn't drive as crazy as they do now.

When I pulled up, Tina came out of the house to talk to me. She stood at the back door of my car while we talked. Out of nowhere, the young girl my friend had been dating, and another chick, ran out of the house and jumped into the back seat, right along with Tina. One of the girls grabbed my hair and started punching me in the head."

"While your son was in the car?"

"Yes, with him in the car."

"What did you do?" Ms. Jones leans in to ask.

"I drove off fast, the back door still wide open, hoping they'd fall out. I started driving in circles, trying to push her off me while making sure I didn't crash. Some guy nearby saw what was happening and yelled for them to get out of my car. Finally, they jumped out, and I sped away.

My son looked at me with watery eyes and asked if I was hurt. I was so mad, mad that a woman I had let into my life would set me up like that and mad for trusting that someone would have my back after always having theirs. She had once been there to protect me from Keith... just to turn around and hurt me too."

Ms. Jones's voice softened. "That is absolutely a reason to feel hurt and betrayed, Nadia. I'm sorry you experienced that, and I don't want to sound like a broken record, but you have gone through some unfair moments in life." She paused for a moment, letting the words sink in. "Speaking of girlfriends… this is before meeting Raya, correct?"

"Yes, I soon started talking to Raya afterwards, which I shouldn't have done."

"Why is that?"

"Well," I said, exhaling, "it was all the drama I was dealing with in my life, as you just mentioned, the unfair moments, and the things I was going through with my children at the time. I had too much on my plate to be worried about relationships."

"What was going on with your kids?" Ms. Jones asks as she writes in her notebook.

"I was moving around so much that I lost everything, beds, dishes, even some pictures. I was homeless again, but my grandma ended up letting us stay with her. She told me I could stay as long as I needed so I could get on my feet, but I was mentally and emotionally all over the place. Looking back, I just wish I had taken a moment to breathe, but life was just happening so fast, and I didn't really know what I was doing." "You had a lot going on."

"Yeah, when we moved into my grandmother's, I called Keith's older cousin and wife, who had mentioned in the past that they would help me with the kids. We spoke on the phone, and eventually I accepted their help and let my kids move out of state to stay with them. I was still in school during all of this, hoping to become better. We were taught that getting a degree would offer stability, so that was the goal. This time, I was going to focus on creating a better life for us. Granted, we all know now that a degree doesn't offer stability, but back then, that was my mission."

Ms. Jones nodded slowly. "That says a lot about you, Nadia, that even while you were drained emotionally, mentally, and financially, you were still trying to push toward a future you believed would provide stability. That takes a lot of strength… but it also takes a lot out of a person." She tilted her head. "Did you have any real support for yourself during that time? Were you at least close with his cousin that you were able to talk about what you were feeling?"

"Not really," I said softly. "But when they found out what was going on, they offered to step in and help me with the kids. At that time, I felt like I had no option but to accept the help."

"That was a blessing to have help at a time you needed it," Ms. Jones said gently. "How did you feel?"

"It was so hard to agree to send my children hours away to live," I admitted. "I felt powerless… like I had failed them as a mother. I know I could have stayed with my grandmother, but if I'm honest, I just felt I needed the break to get it together."

"It takes a strong person to ask for help," she reminded me.

"I didn't feel strong, Ms. Jones," I said, shaking my head. "I had so many mixed emotions during this time… and the whole time, I was worried about how my kids felt."

"Did they understand what was going on?" Ms. Jones asks while jotting in her notebook again.

"No," I said quietly. "My son was four and my daughter two at the time. They were still so young. I told them they would stay with family for a little while so Mommy could get them a new home. The day I dropped them off, I battled with myself, wondering if I was doing the right thing. It was such a hard decision, but I felt like I could get things done faster if they were being taken care of."

"Were you able to focus on school during this time?"

166

"Yes. I continued with school and soon moved in with my second girlfriend, Raya. I would call the kids at least every other day… until my calls went unanswered. I started sending emails, asking what was going on and if everything was okay. Eventually, they responded, telling me it was in the best interest of the children if I didn't speak to them as often."

Ms. Jones's brows wrinkled. "Did you still have legal custody of them?"

"With them living in another state, I had to sign over legal custody. So… no, I no longer had custody of my children. I felt so helpless. And the sad part is, I didn't even have an address for where my children were living."

"What do you mean you didn't have an address?"

I looked down at the floor. "Meaning… they never gave me an address to their place."

"Why wouldn't they tell you where your children were staying?" "I don't know. And sadly, I was so desperate for help, I wasn't noticing those small things at the time. I was just trying to keep going. I was so mad because I felt like there was nothing I could really do… except push harder, hurry, and get them back. I was going to school full-time and working."

I shook my head slowly. "Then one day, I looked over my paycheck stub from one employer… and saw child support being taken out."

Ms. Jones leaned forward slightly. "Was this not part of the agreement?"

"Nope! I was already sending money through MoneyGram to help them out. Now, with child support coming out of my check, I was barely making anything. I was trying so hard, but it felt like I was getting nowhere."

Part Three: Surviving at a Cost

Ms. Jones's pen paused. "What emotions were you feeling in that moment?"

"I wanted to give up," I admitted, my voice cracking. "Nothing in my life was going right. I was taking on extra jobs to save for a 3-bedroom apartment, since they both needed their own room, according to the judge, and losing that much money hurt. I felt hopeless… angry at the world… angry at myself. And, yes… I wanted to give up. And I tried."

Her tone softened. "What did 'giving up' look like for you?"

I let out a bitter laugh. "It looked like shit, I guess. I decided to take a bottle of pills I had just been prescribed for depression. I sat in my car, music blasting, and tossed the first few into my mouth. I cried, begging God to just make everything stop. I didn't want to feel alone anymore… or lost. I popped a few more pills, hoping it would take effect fast, but the music was still pounding in my ears. The world was still there."

"How were you feeling?" Ms. Jones asked gently.

"Empty," I said after a pause. "Like I was still here… but not really here. My body felt heavy, and my head was spinning. I waited to feel numb or pass out, just something other than what I was feeling. I opened my bottled water, dumped all but one pill into it, and shook it until the pills dissolved. I tossed the last pill in my mouth and drank the bottle of dissolved pill water. I waited until the song finished playing, hoping that when the music stopped, so would all the pain."

"You were alone?"

"Yes, in my car... but my girlfriend, Raya, called right after I finished most of the pill water, asking where I was. I told her I wasn't feeling good and was just sitting in the car. I got out and walked into the apartment we shared."

"What happened then?"

"I collapsed onto the couch. She kept asking what was wrong, but I couldn't bring myself to tell her. I didn't want to see the look in her eyes... the disappointment, the pity, the judgment. I just wanted to disappear quietly. I felt like a failure stuck in a damn cycle that wouldn't let me breathe.

I don't remember everything clearly. I think she wanted to talk, but I couldn't stop shaking. She took me to the ER. Things were still kind of blurry from that day. I remember the doctor telling Raya I wasn't going to make it, and the nurse putting something under my nose to keep me awake. I believe they said they couldn't pump my stomach. Hearing my girlfriend cry made me feel so guilty. The next thing I remember is waking up in a hospital room with a stranger watching TV. They told me I was on suicide watch, so someone had to always be in the room with me. That man scared the hell out of me; he looked at me every time I moved in the bed. Honestly, that alone will make you never want to try something like that again."

Ms. Jones set her pen down and leaned forward. "Nadia, let's take a moment to unpack... it sounds like you were carrying more than your body and your mind could hold. It wasn't weakness; it was your body's way of saying, I can't keep going like this. It's a blessing you answered the phone that day and that you walked back inside, and grateful your girlfriend took you to the hospital when she did, and although the man in your room creeped you out, he was there to make sure you were safe."

"I guess, but he still freaked me out, and yeah, I guess I am grateful too."

"Looking back on what happened," Ms. Jones asked gently, "how do you feel now?"

"What do you mean?" I frowned, a little confused by the question.

"You're sitting here telling me about something traumatic from your life," she explained, her voice calm but steady, "and I can feel you holding back some of the emotion. I'm not asking you to relieve the pain, but I'd like for you to tell me, honestly, how that situation made you feel then, and how it makes you feel now, speaking it out loud."

"I feel emotion about things I've been through. I just don't sit around crying about it, as I said before. I don't want people to feel sorry for me. I'd rather keep pushing and hope for something better. So, it's not that I don't feel emotional about things, it's that I can't allow every bad situation to slow me down." "Slow you down from what?" Ms. Jones asked.

"Just… slow me down with the things I want to do in my life. I've been through so much, and I don't want that to be the excuse for why I can't accomplish my goals."

"Showing emotion will not stop you from reaching any goals," Ms. Jones said softly. "Sometimes, it can even help you move toward them faster because you're not carrying all of that weight inside, pretending it's not there. Processing the pain doesn't mean you're weak; it means you're making space for what you want.

You can think of it like emptying your bags to make room instead of trying to stuff it all together."

I sat for a moment before speaking, "Ms. Jones, can I be honest about the question you asked?"

"Yes."

"That day in the hospital… I was scared. I used to think life would be better if I weren't here anymore, but being in that bed opened my eyes. I didn't want to leave the people who were close to me. That time I spent in the hospital gave me time to think."

"What did you think about?"

"I thought about how taking my life would've been selfish… and it took seeing people showing up to visit me to realize that. I was scared there, but I also realized I wasn't as alone as I had convinced myself I was. Almost like I became so lonely with myself that I missed the moments people were actually trying to be there."

"That is a true statement and a great one to reflect on. Are you still feeling lonely now, in your current life, or has that shifted for you?" Ms. Jones asked.

"Can I answer yes, and no?"

"You can answer however you'd like," she said gently, "but I'd like to know the reason for the yes and the no."

"Well, I have some great people in my corner right now, but because of my current situation, I do feel lonely," I admitted, my gaze dropping to my shoes.

Ms. Jones tapped her pen lightly on the pad. "What is it about your current situation that has you feeling lonely?"

I hesitated, feeling the weight of the past mixing with the present. "Are we about to talk about current stuff now?" I asked with a half-smile, trying to lighten the heaviness in the room.

"Yes," she said, her tone soft but intentional. "I think it's time we discuss what's going on in your life right now."

Part Four: She Let Me Fall

"Dasia," I began, letting out a slow breath. "That's my current girlfriend... or maybe my ex. Honestly, I don't even know what we are right now. All I know is we've been fighting, and it's left me feeling lonely. I mean, I know I have people I can lean on, but it's not the same."

"Tell me about her," Ms. Jones said, her tone curious but gentle.

"What do you want to know?"

"Let's start with how you two met."

"I met Dasia online. Don't judge me, but sometimes meeting people online is easier than in public, especially when you don't really hang out in public."

"I'm not judging. A lot of couples meet online now," she replied with a small smile.

"Yes, very true. Well... I was ending another relationship when she and I became friends. She messaged me after reading some poetry I had written and posted on my social media page." "She showed interest in your words, that's sweet."

"I thought so too. We started exchanging messages almost every day. It didn't begin as anything romantic; it was just two people who enjoyed talking, relating, and venting about the relationships we were both dealing with. But over time... it started to feel different. The conversations started to be a part of my everyday.

A morning text, songs she thought I'd like, or that made her think of me."

"You mentioned venting about relationships. Was she still in one?"

"To my understanding, she was not at that time, but looking back, I can't even tell you for sure. We started hanging out, and something sparked. It felt natural and scary all at once, as if it made sense. This sucks to even talk about."

"What sucks?"

"Talking about good stuff when I'm angry with her... it's hard," I admitted. "But she gave me a feeling I'd never felt before, a feeling I thought only existed in fairy tales. Her smile, her laugh... they're perfect. And when she touches me, I swear my whole body just melts. It's crazy. You know how people talk about knowing someone from a past life? I think that's what they mean. It felt like we just... got each other. I started to feel kind of safe with her. Or at least I thought I did." My eyes drifted back down to the floor.

"It sounds like you're in love," Ms. Jones said softly.

"I'd say I was in love," I answered. "But now? I'm not sure what I feel. I found a woman who accepted me for who I was and who I was becoming. She wasn't perfect, and that's what I loved. Her imperfections made her perfect, if that makes sense."

"Yes, she was perfectly imperfect."

"Yeah... something like that," I said with a faint smile. "We could talk about lessons learned and our dreams."

"Lessons learned?" Ms. Jones prompted.

"Just... our pasts. But I was falling, and she told me she would catch me. No, she promised she would catch me, and I believed her. But I hit the floor, and it hurt. She didn't catch me as she said."

"She broke your heart?"

"She shattered it. Some days, it's a dull ache. Other days, it's like a knife twisting when I least expect it, hearing a song, her scent on an old shirt, catching myself reaching for my phone to tell her something. I've never felt pain like the pain she left me with. The stupid part is, she doesn't even get it. She thinks I should just forgive her and keep moving forward. But how do you move forward when all I have to offer are pieces of my heart that she broke?"

Part Five: The Cost of Forgiveness

"The first question you'd need to ask yourself," Ms. Jones said gently, "is, do you forgive her? And beyond that, have you been able to forgive anyone who's hurt you?"

Her words hung between us for a moment. I shifted in my chair, staring at a spot on the carpet as my chest tightened.

"If I forgive them," I finally said, "then it feels like I'm telling that person it was okay they hurt me... like I'm giving them permission to do it again. That's not fair."

Ms. Jones leaned forward slightly, her voice soft but steady. "Forgiveness isn't telling them it was okay. It's saying, 'Yes, you hurt me, but I will be okay.' It's the decision to let that pain stop controlling you. Think of it like this: when you hold on to what they did, you're carrying around a heavy suitcase everywhere you go. Forgiveness is setting that suitcase down. It's giving the pain wings so it can leave you, instead of living in you."

I swallowed hard. "So... if I forgive, I'm not saying it didn't matter?"

"Not at all," she said, shaking her head. "You're saying it mattered, it hurt, but you refuse to let it define you." She tilted her head slightly. "Let me ask you... have you ever done something that hurt someone?"

"I..." I hesitated, staring at my hands like the answer might be written there.

"Have you hurt anyone?" she pressed gently.

175

"Well… yes," I admitted, my voice low. "But I never meant to hurt them."

"Did you ask for forgiveness?"

"Yes," I said quickly. "But I wouldn't keep doing the same thing over and over to hurt that person." I shook my head, feeling the weight of it settle in my chest. "That's the thing, Dasia proved my theory about forgiveness right. I kept forgiving her… and all it did was give her room to keep hurting me. This isn't the first time she's hurt me, but now I just feel stupid for staying. Every time I gave her a clean slate, she painted it with the same mess. When do you stop offering the same person forgiveness?"

Ms. Jones' eyes softened. "Forgiveness is not always for the other person; it's for you. When you hold on to the pain, you also hold on to the version of yourself that was hurt. And that version… doesn't get to grow and heal. Instead, you can get stuck, living in the moment of the wound. Forgiveness lets you move forward, whether that person comes with you or not. And then you determine your boundary by saying enough is enough and walking away."

I let out a bitter laugh. "So, you want me to forgive so I won't be mad anymore?"

"That's one way to put it," she said with a small smile. "We all mess up, we're human. Forgiving someone doesn't mean you accept their behavior or that you must keep them in your life. It means, 'You messed up, and that's part of being human.' Then you choose what's best for you moving forward, without carrying the extra weight of resentment in your bag."

I nodded slowly, though I still felt the resistance in my chest. "I get what you're saying. But to answer your question, no. I don't forgive people. Especially the ones from my past who hurt me and didn't care. It's not in me to just… let that go. But at the same time, I realize I don't have any boundaries either if I keep allowing them to hurt me."

She glanced at the clock before meeting my eyes again. "We're starting to run out of time. I want you to spend some time in between our sessions thinking about what life might look like if you forgave some of the people who have hurt you. Not because they deserve it, but because you deserve peace. Also want you to think about some boundaries that you can put in place to protect that heart of yours."

"Okay," I said reluctantly. "This is going to be hard… but I'll try."

"Trying is a great step," she assured me. "I don't expect you to forgive everyone before our next session. Just picture it. Think about how it might feel to loosen your grip on that suitcase, even for a moment."

"Alright."

She smiled warmly. "I'll see you next time. And remember, do your self-care because you deserve it."

Reflection

Cloud 9

How quietly you crept into my personal space.

Picking up the pieces of my heart and carefully putting them back into place.

You opened my mouth and placed a thousand butterflies inside.

Now my stomach is in constant motion, leaving me giggling all the time.

Not to mention how you send chills up and down my spine, with a simple touch of your hand placed perfectly inside of mine.

You picked me up so swiftly, sat me on a cloud, and sent me up to floor 9.

How quickly do your eyes find me in a crowd just to tell me you're all mine.

So when times get hard between you and me,

Which they will...

...let's agree to try and meet back on floor 9 because hurt can't find us there.

Pass me by, Please!

Slowly, it crept up when I least expected it.

Just like that, it took over my body, and I was put on stage, like some sort of magic show.

I must stand my ground and not lose myself, but it feels so damn good, I can't control myself.

I know too much of it might leave me in pain… damn, I hope this is just a dream…

WOW, the touch is better than I imagined.

How am I going to keep my cool and not later look like a fool?

I'm not ready for this kind of thing.

I've seen the Lifetime movies, and it's all the same.

I don't want to be another chick you can just sweep off her feet and keep it moving, I much rather be that chick that knocks you down on one knee and keep you smiling.

So until then, just let me be, because I sure don't want love walking all over me!

Session Seven

Part One: The Door I Didn't Want to Unlock

I pull up to the building once again and sit in the car, staring at the entrance like it's a choice between breathing and holding my breath. My fingers tighten around the steering wheel. Every part of me wants to start the car and drive away. I don't even have a destination in mind, just the need to vanish.

Somewhere far away where pain doesn't follow, where my cheeks ache from smiling too much. A place where someone takes my hand without asking, pulling me into a dance. Not the kind with heavy bass and grinding bodies, but the slow kind, where they spin me, then draw me close, and we sway together in a rhythm only we can hear. Where we laugh quietly, and they lean in just enough to whisper how beautiful I look.

Does that place exist? Or is it only a sanctuary I build in my head to visit when reality feels too heavy? I sigh, reaching into the backseat for my purse when my phone buzzes.

"Hello."

"Can we meet and talk?" Dasia's voice is cautious, almost rehearsed.

"I don't know if I'm ready for that," I say, eyes fixed on the building's glass doors. "Let me think about it and let you know."
"Okay."

"Okay. Well, I have to go." I hang up before the silence between us can stretch into something I can't handle.

I step inside, greeted by the familiar scent of vanilla oil in a warmer. The receptionist smiles and tells me I can head on back. My steps feel heavier than they should as I walk into Ms. Jones's office and sink into the chair. My gaze drifts to the window, trying to anchor myself to the gray sky beyond.

Ms. Jones sorts through a neat stack of papers before glancing up at me.

"Is everything okay today?" she asks, her voice steady but curious.

"I guess," I said, pulling at a loose thread on my sleeve. "Dasia called as I was walking in and asked if we could talk."

"Oh, okay. Are you ready to talk to her?"

"No."

"That is understandable. How does that make you feel that she wants to talk?"

"I'm... scared."

"Why are you scared?"

"I don't know... I mean, I'm scared of seeing her. What if I forgive her and she hurts me again? What if I don't feel anything at all, which would mean I never really loved her? Or... what if I feel too much and it all comes spilling out in front of her? What if the moment I see her, I can't pretend anymore? No walls, no guard, just everything I've been holding back written all over my face. That would be a mess.

"You are worried that you might not feel anything?"

I shrugged, looking down at my hands. "I'm worried about both. If I feel nothing, it means all the nights I cried, all the pieces of me I gave her, didn't matter. And if I feel everything… it means I'm still not free. That she still has this unexplainable hold on me, and the pain I feel is too much to keep down. I know I will feel something."

"The only way to find out is to talk to her."

"Talk to her about what? How mad am I? How a big part of me regrets everything? How I allowed myself to get lost in this fairytale of what we could be. I don't even know if I can fully call her an ex because I love her so much still, but she's not my girlfriend because I'm so angry at her."

"Are you ready to forgive her?"

I shook my head quickly. "I don't think I am. Can we talk about something else? This topic is making my stomach hurt. Literally." I pressed my hand to my stomach and leaned back on the chair.

"Yes, we can change the subject," she said. "Would you like to pick up where we left off?"

"Sure… what was that?"

"Before we started discussing Dasia, we were talking about you not having your children anymore, and how hard that was for you," Ms. Jones reminded me.

I let out a slow exhale, my eyes fixed on the carpet. "That… was the hardest two years of my life. First, I had to take them to court to get visitation rights. Then, I had to go right back and fight for custody of my own children." My throat tightened, and I swallowed hard. "It felt like I was trapped in this never-ending war, and the enemy was the system that was supposed to protect us."

"What were you feeling during that time?"

"I was confused why they thought keeping my children away from me was best for them," I said quietly. "I am their mother, and I was trying. I may not have been perfect, but I was trying."

"I assume you were able to regain custody because you speak of them in the present," Ms. Jones said.

"Yes," I nodded. "I didn't give up till my babies were home with me." I hesitated, then leaned forward a little. "Can I ask you something?"

"Of course."

"Do you think I keep getting hurt for a reason?"

She tilted her head thoughtfully. "I think you've experienced a lot of pain in your life, and each time, it's taken a piece of you. But let me turn that question back to you, do you think you keep getting hurt for a reason?"

I paused, staring at my hands. "Sometimes… I feel like I'm so broken that even if something 'good' was right in front of me, I wouldn't notice it. Or… when things are good, bad always seems to find me. Just like this past relationship. I don't understand why she would hurt me like she did, especially when I opened up to her about all the pain I've been through before. I shared my trauma and hurt, which I don't normally do… allow anyone in like that."

"Dasia?" she asked gently.

"Yes Dasia."

Part Two: The Weight Behind The Door

"Is that what hurts the most? You opened up to her, and instead of taking care of your pain, you feel she added to the pain?"

Before Ms. Jones could finish the sentence, I dropped my head into my hands, and tears filled my eyes. "Yes! How could she sit and listen to all my hurt while hurting me? I've never opened up to anyone the way I did with her. I allowed her to see me, to see all of me. My ugly that I keep locked away, and she was lying to me. She was cheating on me, and that hurts. If I never gave her so much of me, then this shit wouldn't hurt like it does. We were like a little family. I allowed her to be part of my children's lives, too." I stopped to catch my breath, hoping the tears would stop. "Shit, I can't stop crying."

"Tears are your body's way of expressing the pain and hurt. Allow yourself to show what your heart is feeling." Ms. Jones says, grabbing the box of tissues off her desk.

"But I don't want to feel any of this. It hurts too badly. My heart got it wrong and…I feel so stupid believing love found me. But instead, pain caught back up to me."

"Pain normally doesn't feel good. Don't hide from the pain, allow yourself to feel it."

"Everything hurts," I admitted, clutching the tissue tighter. "I wish I could turn this switch off. Wish I could take back ever meeting her."

"Taking back meeting her would mean taking back even the good memories. Would you want to forget those memories, too? The ones that caused you to fall in love and laugh with each other."

I wipe the tears from my face, the tissue scratching against my skin, and a faint smile tugs at my lips. "No... I'd like to keep those."

"Tell me a good memory you'd like to keep."

"The first one that comes to mind was this one time we were driving in the car," I said, feeling the scene pull me in, "and we were playing songs from all kinds of genres, rap, R&B, even some old-school rock. We didn't care if we knew all the words; we just sang loudly, off-key, laughing when we messed up the lyrics. The windows were down, and the wind blew our hair. For that moment, nothing else mattered... not our past, not the pain. It was just us, in sync with each other, like the world had stopped for a little while so we could be together."

I paused, my smile fading. "I don't know if I'll ever have that kind of ease with someone again. And to have been that close to it... only to lose it? That scares me too."

Ms. Jones nodded slowly, her eyes softening. "That sounds like a memory worth holding onto, and yes, it can be scary not knowing if you will be able to find that type of happiness again, but at least you can say you have experienced it." She let the words hang in the air for a moment before asking, "You two like the same type of music?"

"Yes," I said, the corner of my mouth curling into a small smile. "She loves music as much as I do, it's like... It's how we sometimes spoke to each other. It's how I've always shared my feelings, and she understood. We could go hours sending songs back and forth without saying a word, but somehow, every lyric said exactly what we were feeling." I let out a soft giggle at the thought.

"Sounds like when people would make mix tapes back in the day," Ms. Jones said, her eyes warming.

"Yeah," I nodded. "Except instead of mix tapes, I made CDs. That day in the car… we sang so loud. Neither of us could carry a tune at that moment, but we didn't care. The music was up, the windows were down, and it felt like the world didn't exist beyond that car. We were happy."

"That's a good memory to keep," she said gently. "When you do hurt, remember that moment you felt free, too. Pain hurts, yes… but it also teaches us, shapes us. It helps us grow."

I sighed, my smile fading. "I think I'm tired of growing."

Ms. Jones gave a knowing smile. "I wish it were that easy. But growth doesn't stop, even when we want it to. I continue to learn and grow through pain and mistakes."

"What, not Ms. Jones?" I say with a small giggle, adding a little humor to the tense energy.

Ms. Jones responds with a smile, "Yes, even me. Now that we've visited some of that pain, the question becomes… what do we do with it?"

"I don't know what to do with it," I said, shaking my head as if I could scatter the thoughts away. "It all just hurts. And I doubt anyone is hurting like I am."

"Why do you think that?" Ms. Jones asked, her tone calm but curious.

"Because they caused the hurt. Why would it hurt them? Why say you care for someone only to turn around and do these things to them?"

"It may or may not hurt them," she said gently, "but the truth is… we will never know the full answer to that. And that's okay."

I scoffed under my breath. "Doesn't feel okay. It feels like I'm left holding the weight while they get to walk away lighter. Just like

Crystal... wanting me to call her so she could say, 'Hey, sorry I molested you, I just needed to get it off my chest.' She didn't even take the time to have a real conversation with me about it. She hasn't called since that day." My voice tightened, heat rising in my chest.

"I am so mad at myself for saying, 'It's okay, I forgive you,' because I don't. I don't forgive someone who is that selfish, who can toss something that heavy into my world just to feel better about themselves and then keep it moving. How is that fair?"

Ms. Jones let the silence breathe for a moment, giving the words room to settle. "It isn't fair," she said softly. "And you're allowed to name that. Forgiveness doesn't mean rushing past your pain so someone else can feel comfortable. Sometimes it's about giving yourself permission to stop carrying the responsibility for their choices, even when they never take responsibility themselves."

Part Three: Surviving Myself

"If Crystal were to call you today, what would you say to her?" Ms. Jones asks.

I thought for a moment before I blurted out, "I would tell her that she sucks for taking something away from me." I paused, trying to control all the emotions wanting to rush out of me as if Ms. Jones just asked me to open the flood gates. "I would let her know that I have no idea what type of woman I could have been if I had not experienced being silenced at such a young age. I would tell her that for over 30 years, I thought it was just Frank, and she just called me to say she was the start of it."

I take a deep breath... "I would yell and explain how dirty I felt growing up. And now... I feel angry and sad knowing that two people took from me before I could even speak full sentences. I was just a baby that she took advantage of. I get she went through her own stuff and used me, but dang, she told me how I cried for her to stop, and she didn't. That pisses me off because here I was thinking she would have protected me, only to learn she started the shit. I feel stupid now to think how I thought I looked up to her." I look towards the window, "I would tell her how she hurt me by not even calling back to ask if I was okay. She could have at least asked if I was okay."

"She may never hear those words, but you said them to her. You are releasing it and giving your pain a voice. How about Frank, what would you like to say to him?"

"Frank took away my chance of giving my virginity to someone I chose," I said, my voice tightening. "I will never know when I really lost it, because it was stolen. I was jealous of other girls who could sit in circles and tell their 'first time' stories and laugh. I would pretend mine was with Keith, just so I didn't have to explain the truth. Because honestly… how do you even determine when you lost your virginity when it was taken? It's almost like I never been a virgin if they took from me at 4 fuckin years old."

I felt my nails digging into the tissue in my hand. "I lost my voice because I was scared to speak up. And now, I wonder if I'm antisocial because I had no voice then. I would want to scream at him that it wasn't fair to do that to a little girl… a baby. That I shouldn't have had to grow up hiding in bathtubs to feel safe. Why couldn't playing just be that and not something sexual all the damn time? He made me afraid of my own body before I even understood it."

I swallowed hard, my throat burning. "I would tell him he stole my innocence and replaced it with fear and shame."

Ms. Jones let the silence stretch for a moment. "You're saying it now," she said softly. "Your voice is finally being heard here."

Her words hit something deep, but before I could sit with it, she leaned in a little. "Let's continue. What would you like to say to Keith?"

For a moment, it felt like I could see Keith standing in the room with us as I looked him in the eyes and said, "I was scared you would cause me to take my last breath, but in so many ways, you killed me, emotionally, mentally, and even spiritually. I struggle with relationships because of how unhealthy ours was. I struggle with trust because you lied to me numerous times. I hate how you tried to make me feel stupid when my gut already told me the truth. I wanted my children to have two parents, something I wished for as a child, but you fucked that up. Keith blamed me for taking his family away, yet he destroyed mine. I hated my body and who I was because you told me I wasn't good enough. I jump when things fall because I think it's you coming after me. I wake up screaming in my sleep with the memory of your hands around my neck. You broke the woman I was trying to become, and that hurts in ways I don't even have words for."

Ms. Jones waited a moment before asking, "If you had to speak to one more person who has caused you pain, who would it be?"

My eyes dropped to my lap, my fingers twisting the tissue until it tore. "Dasia," I whispered. "She broke my heart… and now I don't even know how to pick the pieces back up because I'm so tired of mending my heart back together."

The tears came quickly and uninvited. "She didn't just hurt me in the moment; she made me doubt the way I love. She made me question if I'm too much, or not enough, or both at the same time. She knew my past, she knew the scars I carried, and she promised to handle me with care. But instead, she used my vulnerability as a weapon. She took the version of me that was still trying to believe in love and smashed it into pieces so small I can't even see them all to put them back together."

I pressed the tissue to my eyes, hoping to stop the tears that were flowing out. "I feel like everything I've been through, Frank, Crystal, Keith, all of it already broke me, but Dasia…" My voice cracked. "She's the one who made me afraid even to try again. Ms. Jones, she hurt me that I had to come speak to you because I couldn't go to the hospital for this pain. No offense to you, but if she had never hurt me, I wouldn't be here now, unable to control my emotions."

Ms. Jones leaned back, her eyes steady on mine. "That's a heavy door you just opened, Nadia. But I am glad you are pushing through and saying what you feel." She paused, letting her words sink in. "She hurt you because you trusted her with your heart. You've been looking for safety for most of your life. And when she couldn't fill that emptiness, it cut deep. Sometimes the hardest truth is accepting that people aren't perfect... and that love always carries the risk of pain."

"Does that mean it was okay for her to hurt me?"

"No. Not at all. It means that with love, we allow someone the power to hurt us, hoping they never will." She tilted her head slightly, softening her tone. "Before we move on, I have to ask, have you thought about what forgiveness might look like for you?"

Part Four: The Weight Behind the Door

"I tried to think about it, but it made me mad again. Why do I need to forgive people who hurt me? I'm still not understanding."

"That is okay. You do not have to forgive them right now, but I'm glad you thought about it," Ms. Jones says gently. "I think we won't focus on the forgiveness topic at this moment. Let's talk about how you felt expressing your feelings to the people who have hurt you?"

I looked out the window at a bird sitting on a nearby tree branch. Its wings twitch, like it's deciding whether to stay or fly. Again, I wished that I were that bird, free to leave, free to go anywhere. Just being part of the Earth rather than having to be in it to this degree.

I look at Ms. Jones, who is patiently waiting for me to reply. "I guess... it felt good," I admit. "I almost feel like I was able to tell them how I felt, even without them here."

"Sometimes," Ms. Jones nods, "we don't need the person in our presence to tell them how we feel because sometimes those people just aren't on the same growth process with you. Meaning they aren't able to be present when we are ready to release and heal, so you improvise."

"I would have never thought of doing that," I say, shaking my head. "I do feel a little better. Plus, it's nice not having to look them in the face, because... who knows what I could do with this anger." I say with a small smirk while shrugging my shoulders, but the truth is, I'm not a fighter; hell, I'm just now learning to fight for myself without feeling guilty.

Still, I've had moments where I thought of packing up my car with my kids and just driving off, like I've seen women do in movies, starting over somewhere new. But then I always worried all my baggage would still find me, and it would be the same shit, just a new scenery.

The bird outside flies off, and I watch it disappear into the sky. My mind follows it, imagining where I would go if I could fly away from everything. My safe place has always been near water. The ocean feels like home, like it could wash away the heaviness I carry. I picture Virginia, a place I've never lived but always felt a pull toward. The sound of waves, the endless horizon... somehow, I believe I'd be free there and maybe finally feel at home.

"You don't realize how much strength it took for you to do what you just did," Ms. Jones says softly. "That was you unlocking the door you didn't want to face. You let yourself speak, and you allowed a part of you to be free."

I nod slowly, wiping my eyes. "Maybe, but I don't feel free yet."

"It will take some time." Ms. Jones continues. "I would like for us to pause here for now and take some deep breaths. Next session, I would like for us to talk about forgiveness and what that looks and even feels like for you. Also, let's talk about some things you are proud of."

"Things I'm proud of?"

"Yes. Take some time to think about the positives of who you are for the next session. Through all that you have been through, I can only imagine what you have learned, and I'm sure there are things in there that have kept you going. Enjoy the rest of your day and remember to do some self-care."

"I will try. See you next session, and thank you, Ms. Jones."

As I stand to walk out of her office, I glance back at the window. The bird is gone. The sky is wide open, and I imagine it soaring toward the shore I've only seen in dreams. Maybe one day, I'll find my way there too, I think to myself.

Reflection

Love is...

Love is something so hard to explain

Something you wish would always stay

How to say, "I love you,"

And not have you run away.

How to say, "I need you," And not be too lame.

Love is the strangest thing.

Session 8

Part One: Life Beyond Survival

"Hello, how did your week go?" Ms. Jones asks as I walk in.

"It went well," I say, sitting down in the chair.

"How are you feeling?"

"I feel emotionally drained, to be honest. I had time to think about forgiveness and stuff."

"Would you like to discuss what you were thinking about?"

I sigh, pressing my hands into my lap. "I thought about how I would feel if I forgave those who have hurt me. As much as I want to forgive and move on with my life, it scares me. I don't think forgiving them will fix how I feel."

"You're right, forgiving isn't going to fix what you're feeling," Ms. Jones says calmly, "but it can help you move forward."

I stare down at the carpet, tracing the patterns with my eyes. "But what if I forgive them, and it makes me look weak? What if forgiving means they got away with what they did to me?"

"Forgiveness isn't about letting them get away with anything," she explains. "It's about releasing the hold their actions still have on you. It's giving yourself permission to carry less of that weight."

I feel my throat tighten. "It feels like I've been carrying so much weight for so long… I don't even know what life would feel like without it."

"Does living without all the anger scare you?"

"I never thought of it that way."

"Take a moment and ask yourself, can you live without the anger, so you can forgive and move forward?"

Her words drift over me, and for a moment, I close my eyes to picture waking up one morning without the heaviness I've always carried. No bitterness in my chest, no shame pressing on me, and no wall keeping me from fully loving. Just me, waking up smiling and being grateful for the day. The sound of my kids laughing in the background fills the house with joy. For one small second, I feel peace, and it feels so good it hurts.

Then the vision fades, and fear pulls me back like a rope around my waist. That kind of life doesn't happen to women like me. That's movie stuff, make-believe endings. I open my eyes and shake my head slightly, pushing the thought away before asking Ms. Jones. "Will that change me as a person? It's like all I know how to do is survive. What does living even feel like?"

"I think many people have lived with anger, hurt, or pain for so long that living without it can feel very different. The emotion has been with someone so long that it almost becomes part of them."

"I am curious to know if letting go of the anger will create a different person?"

"Who are you now?" Ms. Jones looks at me and asks.

"What do you mean?"

"Who are you as a person now?"

Part Two: Who Am I

The room feels quieter than usual, almost like it's waiting on me to speak first. Ms. Jones studies me for a moment, then gently asks again, "Who are you now?"

Her question lingers in the air. My throat feels tight, and for a moment, I don't even know how to begin. Who am I? For so long, I've known myself only by what I've survived. Hurt. Anger. Survival. That's been my definition. But without all that, who is left?

I take a slow breath and repeat the words out loud. "Who am I?" The question feels strange on my tongue, almost foreign. I hesitated, but then I spoke. "I am quiet...shy is what I've been told. Umm… I am determined. I believe I have a good heart." "Tell me more about who you are," Ms. Jones encourages.

I stare at my hands in my lap, searching for something solid to hold onto. "I was able to accomplish my degree during all of this, which I still can't believe."

She nods softly. "And that explains your determination. What else?"

My voice steadies as I push through the uncertainty. "I enjoy helping people, which I guess shows I'm caring, but I can be moody too. I think I am a good mother, friend, sister, and daughter. I think I can be a good partner if someone is willing to love me in return. I am loving and understanding. I am sad because of my past, but I am hopeful for a happy ending one day. I love making people laugh and smile, so I would consider myself a funny person. Sadly, I laugh at my own jokes too." I say with a small giggle.

Ms. Jones leans in slightly. "Now, if you take out the anger that has been in your life, do you think that would change any of what you described?"

"I guess not feeling angry wouldn't change who I am as a person, but it might change how I look at things."

"I think you're right," Ms. Jones responds repeat in my head. "The anger doesn't define you as a person, but releasing it could allow you to see life through a different lens."

I sat quietly, letting her words settle. "I can say I already view life differently now, especially since I was diagnosed with an autoimmune disease. Instead of fighting to give up my life, I fight for my life."

Her expression softens. "You have an autoimmune disease? I'm so sorry to hear that."

"Yes." I nod, remembering the day everything shifted. "It's something I'm still learning to live with. I found out a few years ago when I woke up, and the whole room was spinning. I couldn't walk straight. I'd bump into walls, stumble into furniture, and sometimes fall down the stairs. I thought I was losing my mind." My voice lowers as I reflect on the truth.

"I was going to have to choose life, no matter how hard it was. But the doctors picked and poked at me until finally they gave me a name for it, an autoimmune disease. I left with more questions than answers, but one thing I knew for sure: my body was demanding I start fighting in a new way."

I pause, staring out for a moment. "That was the day I realized I wasn't just surviving anymore. I was going to have to choose life, no matter how hard it was."

I take a breath. "I guess this is where I need to choose life, not just physically, but mentally and emotionally too? For so long, I've fought to survive what was done to me. Where survival meant staying guarded, always bracing for the next impact. It meant shrinking parts of myself or struggling to get out of bed just to make it through the day. I learned how to take what was given, not how to live. Somewhere along the way, I forgot that there could be more to me. I didn't just have to accept; I was allowed to create what I wanted. Now I get to fight for who I'm becoming."

Ms. Jones smiles at me, "You are getting it now. You are so much more than you have given yourself credit for, and I am so thankful you are allowing me to be part of this growth with you."

I look out the window, hoping to see the bird, but it's gone. Maybe it's on a new journey. Maybe, just like me, it's learning to spread its wings to fly. I reflect on Ms. Jones' words about being part of my growth and exhale. I met Ms. Jones with eye contact, and I said, "I guess who I am is strength, and growth, and learning to become more than I was."

Ms. Jones nods, "Beautiful!"

Part Three: Surviving Myself

Ms. Jones jots some notes in her notepad, then looks up at me.

"If you don't mind me asking, did the doctors tell you what type of autoimmune disease?"

"I don't mind. Most of my doctors say lupus, but I have one doctor who isn't ready to put that on paper, so officially it just says autoimmune disease. Lupus is such a tricky thing to diagnose, but I have most of the symptoms."

"What are the symptoms you are dealing with?"

I let out a breath, pressing my fingers together. "I've had swollen joints, organs that seem to act stupid at times, headaches almost every day, and the sun irritates me if I'm out too long. Some mornings, I'm so tired I can't get out of bed, but I push myself because life and bills don't stop for me. Stress makes it worse, go figure… sucks when my whole life was built on stress. And don't forget teenagers," I add with a half-smile.

We both chuckle softly, but the laughter fades. My chest tightens as I continue.

"Sometimes it feels like I'm trapped inside a body that doesn't want me. It feels like it's betraying me when I need it most. I don't want my kids to see me weak, so I pretend I'm fine while cooking dinner with swollen hands, hiding the tears when I can't carry the laundry or groceries, pushing through headaches so I can help with homework. They don't deserve to carry my pain." The words sit heavy between us. I rub my palms against my knees, voice softer now.

"I used to think surviving was my strength, but surviving like this feels different. It's not just surviving the world or the people who hurt me. It's surviving myself. My own body."

My throat tightens, and I swallow hard. "Some days I wonder, am I just someone sick now? Or am I still the determined, strong woman I fought to be? I don't want to be remembered as the sick mom. I want my kids to look back and remember my strength, my love, not my pain."

For a second, my eyes blur with tears. "But sometimes... they're the only reason I get out of bed. When I hear them laughing in the kitchen, mainly arguing, I think, this is why I'm still here. Even when my body wants to quit, they're my anchor. They're the reason I drag myself up when all I want to do is stay down."

I pause, staring at the floor. "And yet, part of me wonders if maybe my body breaking down was the only way I'd finally stop carrying everything else. It forced me to pay attention. It was a wake-up call... and now, I try to be grateful for the days I wake up without pain, for the chance to still be here. I'd rather struggle through another day than not have a chance to try at all."

Ms. Jones studies me with kind eyes. "Life has a way of opening our eyes sometimes. Not allowing heaviness to dictate every part of our lives. I'm glad you have found a way to live through some of what you are carrying to look at it gratefully."

I let out a half-laugh. "Ms. Jones, I have a feeling we're going back to me needing to forgive again."

Part Four: Unlocking The First Door

"Since you are bringing it up, why not discuss forgiveness?" Ms. Jones asked with a gentle smile.

"Okay. Yes, I should forgive so I can heal, but forgiving people sucks." I glanced toward the window, my jaw tightening. We both just sat in silence for a few minutes, so that even the clock seemed loud.

"What are you thinking?" Ms. Jones finally asked, her tone calm.

"I was trying to picture my life without anger," I admitted slowly. "And honestly... it seems freeing. Just because I forgive these people doesn't mean I have to talk to them, right?"

"No, not at all," Ms. Jones replied. "Forgiving is something for you, not for them. Forgiveness is part of healing, and healing is what allows you to grow."

I twisted the tissue in my hand until it was nothing but a crumpled knot. "I want to forgive Dasia because I love her, but I don't want her to think she can lie to me again. If I forgive her, does that mean I have to be with her again? I want to forgive my past because I'm ready to live in the present. I want to move forward with my future. But right now, I feel like I'm tied down with all these negative feelings. They're heavy, like anchors I can't pull up."

Ms. Jones leaned forward slightly. "Forgiving Dasia, or anyone else, doesn't mean going back. It doesn't mean excusing what they did. It means loosening the grip their choices still have on you. Forgiveness doesn't force reconciliation; it simply frees you."

I swallowed hard. "But if I let go of this anger, then what? This anger feels like the only thing protecting me. It's my way of saying, 'No, it wasn't okay.' If I put it down, won't that mean it was, okay?"

Her eyes softened. "That's a powerful point. Sometimes anger feels like armor, a way to keep your heart safe. But carrying it for too long ties knots in your gut. Those knots get tighter every time you relive the hurt, and instead of protecting you, the anger ends up choking you. What if forgiveness wasn't about saying 'it's okay', but about untying those knots, giving your heart the space to breathe?"

I pressed the tissue to my lips; my chest was aching. "I don't even know if I can imagine that. Anger has been my way of surviving. Without it… I don't know who I'd be. It's almost like it's all I have to show that what they did was wrong."

"And yet," Ms. Jones said gently, "here you are, strong enough to name it, strong enough to say it out loud. That means you are already more than your anger. Anger is a statement, yes, but it doesn't have to be your only language. What if protecting your heart didn't mean holding on so tightly, but learning to trust yourself enough to let go?"

The room went quiet again. My shoulders sagged as her words settled into me, heavy and light all at once. For the first time, I wondered if maybe the anger wasn't saving me; it was holding me hostage. "I'm tired of feeling tied down with so many negative emotions," I say softly.

"Forgiving will not happen overnight, but it will be a process of putting one foot in front of the other," Ms. Jones said, her tone steady but encouraging. "If you forgive Dasia, it is still your choice whether you want the relationship or not. Forgiveness does not bind you to anyone; it sets you free. Let's start by you telling me out loud that you are ready to try and forgive."

I swallowed hard, my palms damp as if I were holding the words instead of my hands. For a moment, my throat locked up. Saying it

204

out loud meant admitting I was ready to loosen the grip I'd held onto for so long.

"Okay." My voice trembled. "Well, Ms. Jones…" I took a breath so deep it made me lightheaded on the way out. "I think I am ready to forgive those who have hurt me. I am ready to forgive myself for believing I deserved to stay stuck in all that pain. I want to try and forgive… so I can finally be free from that heaviness. I want to live a life where I'm free, not holding on to all the hurt and pain." Tears rolled down my cheeks, but for once, they didn't feel heavy. And yet… even as I said it, I felt a strange ache. Not for the past. Not for Dasia. But for something I couldn't name yet. Like my heart knew there was something else coming, but I needed to release this part of me first.

Ms. Jones smiled softly, her eyes meeting mine with a quiet strength. "That's a powerful step, Nadia. You've just spoken freedom into existence. You've unlocked the first door. Now the journey begins."

"Thank you."

Part Five: Stepping into the Light

"No one deserves to stay in a negative place. We grow from the past, not live every day in it. Sometimes the first step is just talking to someone about it."

"I agree. You encouraged me well, more so, pushed me to start talking. I know I've made it hard to open up, but just talking about what's hurt me in the past makes me feel less angry. It feels like a weight has lifted off me by simply talking to you."

"People find it hard to talk to a therapist or anyone safe, but it can be helpful." Ms. Jones, with a soft smile.

"I did have a hard time sharing my personal life with you at first, but it feels nice now." I pause and glance around the room before asking. "Do we still need to meet? Are you going to say I need medicine? I don't like taking any medications. It's hard for me to take medicine for a cold." I say with a quick laugh.

"I would like to continue meeting with you, but not as often. If you feel comfortable and up to it, you could suggest to Dasia that she should come in with you for a session."

"I haven't even built up the nerve to talk to her."

"It is just a suggestion if you decide to work through the hurt. It might be easier to talk with a third-party present. Sometimes it's helpful to navigate through the conversation to make sure each person is being encouraged to be heard."

"That makes sense. Thank you, Ms. Jones. I think I will talk to her, but I'm going to take some time to forgive her first. Just to make sure I am in a space where I can hear her without the anger presenting me first."

"That sounds like a plan. I want to encourage you to make some time for self-care, and we should plan to meet again in a few weeks for a follow-up. But if you feel the need to meet sooner, you are more than welcome to schedule before that."

"What is next for me? What does tomorrow look like now?"

"When you can start forgiving, it gives you a chance to accept today and prepare for tomorrow. What you do next is breathe! Tell yourself that you are okay despite what you went through. Who you were was because of yesterday, but who you are is shaped by how you made it through yesterday. Everything is going to be okay."

"Thank you, Ms. Jones, and I am going to be okay today."

I grab my purse and stand up. As I leave the building, the warm sun hits my face, and I smile. For the first time in a long time, the sunlight doesn't feel heavy on my skin; it feels like it's been waiting for me. Like it knew I had finally made space for its warmth.

I take a deep breath, the air filling my lungs with something I haven't felt in years: possibility.

I feel like I left behind some of the baggage I've been carrying for so long. I walked into therapy with what felt like an entire suitcase full of pain, shame, and anger, yet I'm leaving with just my purse. It's still messy inside, some emotions still need sorting, but it's no longer weighing me down.

And maybe that's what healing looks like. Not dropping everything all at once, but lightening the load piece by piece. I walk toward my car, and this walk feels different, lighter. I look up and sitting right there on the hood of my car is the same little bird I'd noticed in past sessions. For a moment, I just stand still, watching it tilt its head at me as if it knows something I don't. Almost like it's waiting.

I smile softly through fresh tears. Weeks ago, I wished I could be like that bird, free, able to fly anywhere, far from the weight of my past. And now here it is, perched at the very place I have to step into to move forward. Maybe it's not here to remind me of escape, but to remind me that freedom doesn't mean running away. Sometimes freedom is choosing to stay and live differently.

The bird flutters its wings and takes off into the sky, going to their next adventure, and I whisper to myself as I slide into the driver's seat, "Something inside me woke up… and I don't know what it means yet, but I'm going to find out what's next."

What came next wouldn't arrive all at once,

But it was already on its way.

Reflection

Hello Love...

Today I was introduced to a new kind of love.

A love that I've heard about and wished upon a star for.

The kind of love that comes once in a lifetime.

I woke in the arms of love.

I made breakfast for love and smiled.

Love watched me shower, then rubbed lotion on my body.

I went to the park and laughed with love.

Love listened as I spoke.

Love held me as I watched the sunset.

Love still loved after hearing my secrets.

Love didn't judge my flaws but embraced my strengths and accepted my weaknesses.

Love kissed the pain and wiped away the tears.

Love is my hero for my fears.

Love made a candlelight dinner and rubbed the stress out of my feet.

Love held me as I slept.

Today I introduced myself to self-love.

And for the first time, I realized my heart was finally open... open to

something more than survival, open to something I haven't met yet,

But I feel it's coming... Love is preparing me!